I0824430

The Demons of the Blood

A Metrognomes Adventure

Also by Glenn Slade Clark, Jr.

Cry, Wolf: Shadow of the Werewolf

THE CHRONICLES OF NIGHTFIRE, TEXAS:

The Vampire Murders

The Haunting of Alexas Mansion

The Great Debate

Metrognomes: The Shaman's Apprentice

The Demons of the Blood

A Metrognomes Adventure

Glenn Slade Clark, Jr.

Illustrated by Paige Carpenter

2016

The Demons of the Blood: A Metrognomes Adventure

First Edition: October 2016

Published by Clark Ink, LLC.

Cover art and illustrations by Paige Carpenter.

ISBN-10: 1-61815-124-X

ISBN-13: 978-1-61815-124-7

Some of us see our scars and remember that we were wounded; others of us see our scars and remember that we survived.

This book is for the survivors.

Contents

TIMELINE OF THE METROGNOMES UNIVERSE

1,052 TQ

The Demons of the Blood: A Metrognomes Adventure

1,061 TQ

Music of the Metrognomes (short story)

1,066 TQ

Metrognomes: Worse than a Gremlin (short story)

Metrognomes: The Shaman's Apprentice

Dates on this timeline represent the years of Tribe Qadash (TQ), from the Qadash Grand Calendar. An up to date timeline is maintained at www.GlennSladeClarkJr.com.

THE DEMONS OF THE BLOOD

A METROGNOMES ADVENTURE

1
Xersek the Exorcist

The gnome shaman Xersek climbed down from the back of the great war armadillo, that had carried him all the way from the caverns of Tribe Riven, and approached the home of his old friend Malík, which was cleverly hidden beneath the root of the great tree that guarded Malík's appointed tribe. Xersek found the door, which to an untrained eye blended perfectly with the bark of

the tree root itself, and he made three distinct knocks upon it with the head of his staff.

Malík opened the door, the white hair of his long beard disheveled, stains and fresh globs of soft food on his robe. This was not the usual well-kept appearance of the powerful shaman Xersek had been dear friends with for more than two hundred years.

Malík took in the sight of the younger shaman at his door, the urgent look on his face, the war armadillo behind him. "Xersek! What a surprise. Please come in, my friend."

Xersek nodded, and he wasted no time in entering the little home. He took in the sight of the place, which was just under a year old but looked as though it had been lived in for decades. The books on the shelves, which Malík had always been fastidious about keeping in order, were stacked akimbo, leaning against one another in disarray; there were dishes unwashed on the counter, fairy powder was spilled in a great pile on the floor, and Malík himself looked as though he had been struggling to catch his breath. "Malík, are you well?" Xersek asked with visible concern.

Malík began to see himself through Xersek's eyes then, and he laughed. "Oh, I'm fine, old friend. I'm fine. It's just been one of those years, you know." A haunted look colored the old gnome's face. "A year I hope never to see the like of again."

A baby crying caught Xersek's attention, and he took in a sharp breath, smiling at himself for having forgotten such an important detail. "Malík! I was so caught up with urgent matters of my own that I had forgotten your new apprentice!" He followed the sound of the baby's voice to a cradle behind a stack of books, and he reached in to pick the child up, taking in the sight of him as a wonder.

The baby stopped crying and studied the new face, looking confused. This was not Malík.

Suddenly the baby giggled, and Xersek giggled back, turning to Malík. "Is it true? All that I've heard about him? The circumstances of his discovery?"

"If what you have heard seems far-fetched, then yes. The child is exactly what I have said he is, and he comes from exactly where you have heard." Malík grinned proudly, beaming as he watched his friend hold the infant before him.

"And what is it you call him?"

"Ak'ten," Malík said. "And he's quite the handful."

"Oh!" Xersek agreed, "I imagine so! A magical baby, on top of relocating your entire tribe, picking yourselves up after that Darkgnome catastrophe, building a new cavern system here in Gremlin territory! No wonder you're …" He looked the older shaman up and down, "… in such a state. I'm sorry I haven't been in touch more these past months. I should have come by sooner. Oh, look at you, Malík!"

"Yes, well…" Malík cleared his throat and reclaimed his composure, wiping his hands fruitlessly over a few choice baby food stains on his robes. "What brings you by, old friend? You had mentioned some urgent matters of your own."

"Yes." The shadow returned to Xersek's face, framed by his long, brown beard and earth-colored skull cap. Gently, he put the baby back into the cradle. "I'm afraid we're having dark problems of the sort only shamans can attend to, in Tribe Riven. I need your help, Malík."

"What is it, Xersek? Of course I'll do whatever I can."

"My tribe has been recently terrorized by an absolute horror from the nether realm. Lives have been lost. So much blood, Malík. It was something out of myth. Something I never dared dream could come back to harm us. And I, an expert on demons."

"What happened?"

Xersek found a chair and took a seat, gripping his staff as though it could protect him from the story he was about to tell.

Malík noticed that the shadowy countenance of his friend was much more pronounced than normal. Xersek could be grim, even severe, compared to some of the other shamans. In fact, most of the other shamans in the Collective considered Xersek an unsettling, even spooky apparition, and they were loath to deal with him except in times of crisis. Malík knew a softer side of the old demonologist, but even he was frightened by the fear on Xersek's face.

"Our builders had been digging, in the Royal Caverns," Xersek began, "adding a new level to the great family tree. It had been centuries since such a project had been necessary, you know, but over the course of four thousand years, we have, on occasion, run out of room on the wall, and it becomes necessary to add another level, deeper in the earth.

"The gods know how long they had been buried there, Malík. Five thousand years at least. They're real, Malík. All the legends are true."

"What's real? What are you talking about?"

"The Demons of the Blood. They were buried beneath the Royal Caverns of Tribe Riven long before the tribe even existed. And … we freed them, Malík."

Malík was stunned. "By the gods! I've always thought that a bedtime story. I've never encountered any spirit that behaved as they are said to behave. Are you sure?"

"Malík," a chilling gleam shone from the eyes of the consummate demonologist, "I am sure. As you know, there are six chiefs among the Demons of the Blood, and countless followers within their dark clan. The chiefs can possess the dead, raise them up again, and begin to pass the possession on to their families."

"I have to admit," Malík said, "I'm not sure exactly how they operate. I remember the basic story, but I'm a fairy expert. Demons are your department, Xersek. Tell me everything, as though I knew nothing."

Xersek nodded. He removed a thick book from the deep inside pocket of his robe and stood, going to the table and clearing away dirty bowls and cups in order to set it down and open it.

Malík went to stand beside him, as he turned the pages. It was a book of atrocities from the First Time, a book that surely only one such as Xersek would have ever had the heart to read. "I recognize this book," Malík said. "Io spoke of it, long ago."

Another nod from Xersek. "Yes. *The Necromancy of Gothos*. I spent fifty years in pursuit of it, thinking I was learning about the distant past; never suspecting I was preparing for the future. The earliest copies are scrolls, dating back ten thousand years. This particular codex is about six hundred years old, and it's probably one of the latest copies in existence. The book was banned in many tribes around the time that this copy was created. It was considered evil in itself for the terrible things that it contains. But you and I both know that knowledge is never evil, even knowledge *about* evil. Knowledge is a light in the dark, and we, as shamans, value nothing else above the light."

He pointed to an etching that filled the entirety of the right page, clearly illustrating the Demons of the Blood in their violent fervor. "Six chiefs, as I said. The first can possess any corpse it chooses, so long as the body has living offspring in the world. The possessed corpse then begins to pump blood through the body's veins once again, and the other five chiefs can go on to possess other related corpses. Cousins, siblings, and so on, as long as the bodies have living offspring. Hence the moniker 'Demons of the Blood.'

"Once the six chiefs are in place, they begin seeking out their host bodies' descendants, both living and dead. Father or mother will find son or daughter and force the gnome to drink blood from the parent's possessed veins. This allows one of the countless demons in the infernal clan to come forth and possess the gnome who has drunk the blood, and then that demon seeks out the next in line of descent. When they've exhausted a line, the chiefs can jump at any time into another cousin and bring forth more demons. In this way, the Demons of the Blood could take over an *entire* gnome tribe, as all clans within the tribe are ultimately cousins to one another, descending from the thirteen sons of the tribe's first king.

"The only limitation the demons have is that they cannot possess anygnome who is without child. But that does not mean such gnomes are spared. The demons revel in bloodsport, they feast on blood, they bathe in blood, and they hold the childless they leave alive like livestock, to be bred, to provide more bodies over time. Enough to bring forth the entire demon clan. This is exactly what has happened within the royal clan of Riven."

Malík had gone very pale. "Xersek, I'm so sorry."

Dismissing the sentiment with a weary nod, Xersek went on, "When the builders accidentally released the demons from their prison, the first chief went immediately to the royal tombs and resurrected the body of King Thanatos, who had died just last year. The other five chiefs followed his lead and made their assault on Clan Riven. Thanatos sought out his son, King Soma to make him drink the blood, and the deed was done. Imagine the horror, Malík. Before I could even discern what we were up against, these ancient nightmares had already taken control of the tribe through our reigning king!

"I warned our warriors against dealing any fatal blows, and while some warriors, distant cousins to the royal clan, were taken by the chiefs, the rest managed to help me drive out the demons, but not before they took the crown prince's young son, Prince Lumino, hostage.

"I put a protection against them up around the royal caverns, then we sealed the entrances to the larger tunnel system against them.

"They demanded that Prince Infractus come in person to retrieve his son. While his father remains possessed, Infractus is effectively the ruler of the tribe. If they can take him, they will have Tribe Riven fully under their sway.

"I told Prince Infractus that I would set out alone and vanquish the demons, returning them to imprisonment. I promised to return his son and his father, but I could not take any warriors from Tribe Riven with me, for fear they would be possessed by the demon chiefs.

"That is why I've come to you, old friend. I fear this ancient evil may overwhelm me. I need help, and a warrior's presence would be welcome as well, if your tribe has any to spare in these dark times of war against the Gremlins. I need the help of gnomes who are not related to Tribe Riven."

Malík nodded somberly. "Of course, my power is your power, Xersek, and I know of a warrior we may be able to ask to join us, but are you sure we are safe?"

"What do you mean?"

"Aren't all gnomes ultimately related, as a species? We may have different tribes, different clans, and different skins, but aren't we all descendants of the first gnomes?"

"A clever point, Malík, but demons are funny creatures. They operate by rules, some of them less than rational. They are magical and superstitious beings. I am only beginning to crack the mystery of their origin as a whole, but I do know that every brand of demon believes in certain universal rules of their existence. Names have great power over them, for one. And with this particular legion, if a family connection is not remembered, these blood demons cannot exploit it. In other words, it is the very family tree of the tribe, which we were building another level to, that has provided them with their blueprint for conquest. They are unconcerned with the species connection as a whole. They know only the bloodline that is recorded on the great wall that begins with King Aleph Riven, three thousand nine hundred ninety-nine years before the reign of King Soma. This means that you and I, and any warrior from Tribe Qadash who may accompany us, are safe from possession. It is detailed here, in the *Necromancy*."

"That's good to know," Malík said with relief.

"Oh, does it comfort you, Malík, to know that all we need fear is being torn to pieces; our blood used to fill their goblets and to bathe their stolen skins?"

Remembering suddenly why Xersek was seldom invited to dinner parties, Malík answered somberly, "I see your point, Xersek. We must proceed with all caution. There is only one warrior currently home on leave from the entire Qadash army. But as warriors go, we could hope for no better. He's quite renowned, even considered a candidate for the next Qadash general, and hailing from a long line of legendary warriors."

"Oh? And who is this?"

"Scarro Jinto. He is home at the request of Clan Jinto's venerable patriarch, Methule, who wanted their mightiest warrior at his table for the week of festivities surrounding his one hundred tenth birthday. Incidentally, the festival week ended two days ago, but the general granted Scarro two weeks leave, so that he might spend some time with his wife and son before returning to the battlefield."

"Scarro Jinto," Xersek mused. "I know the name. I have heard of his part in saving your tribe from the uprising last year. And I hear from our own warriors how he and his apprentice are marvels on the battlefield against the Gremlins. I feel badly taking him from his family, though. Did I hear you correctly, that his patriarch turned one hundred ten?"

"Yes. Methule is the oldest clan patriarch in the history of Tribe Qadash."

"Very impressive. I've never known a gnome other than a shaman to live so long. And *we* cheat."

Malík laughed lightly at this. They did cheat at that. "And I hate to take Scarro from his family too," he agreed, "but I know he will not hesitate to go. It is his nature. You'll find him a very grim gnome. He's only thirty-five, but you would think he had seen a thousand years of war. He puts the warrior life above all."

"That sounds … sad," Xersek said.

"I think it must be." Malík nodded thoughtfully. "But he knows no better. His family has been that way for generations. I'm just saying that he will have no qualms about joining your quest, especially as the only warrior available."

"Oh for the love of the gods!" Xersek backed away suddenly in horror.

Malík's heart skipped a beat. Sudden fear pierced his very being to see the demonologist who had seen countless terrible things shrink back in horror himself. He heard Ak'ten giggling furiously behind him. "What is it?" he looked around, calling his magic staff to his hand telekinetically to fend off whatever evil had joined them in his home.

Xersek's nose scrunched up, and he covered it, backing away towards the door. "I believe your apprentice has dropped a stink bomb of unholy proportions. And he seems to think it's funny! I shall await you outside while you change him."

"Oh, yes," Malík said sourly. "I smell what you're saying." He turned, holding his nose, to regard the laughing baby. "And I assure you, he *does* think it's funny."

2
The Warrior's Hearth

Once Ak'ten was cleaned and changed and bundled in Malík's arms, the two shamans made their way to the main entrance of Tribe Qadash's cavern system, where they were allowed past the two guards on Malík's authority. Xersek's armadillo was far too large to carry them into the tunnels, so they made their way on foot, through the long entry corridor, through the market square, through the gates of Clan Jinto's caverns, and all the way to the home of Scarro Jinto, where Malík knocked upon the door.

The door opened to the bright, smiling face of Scarro's wife Melendie. "Malík!" she greeted him merrily. "Come in!"

The shamans both obliged. "Melendie, this is Xersek," Malík gestured with his head, "shaman of Tribe Riven."

The two newly acquainted gnomes exchanged pleasantries, then Melendie moved close enough to Malík to offer the sleeping baby in his arms her finger, which the child gripped both absently and tightly. "Oh, I just love Ak'ten," she cooed. "He's so sweet."

"Well," Xersek grumbled playfully, "his sense of humor leaves something to be desired."

Melendie laughed. "He's just a baby. He doesn't have a sense of humor yet."

"Yes he does," both shamans said in unison.

As if on cue, Ak'ten woke up, broke wind, and giggled.

"Who is it, Mother?"

All eyes turned to the ten-year-old boy who had joined them in the entryway. "Jono, this is Xersek, one of Malík's shaman friends."

Jono sized up the brown-bearded shaman and laughed. "He's creepy."

"Jono!" Melendie scolded, but she could not keep the amusement from her voice. Then she added, in a concerned whisper, "Your father would not approve."

Malík cleared his throat, subtly reclaiming Melendie's attention. "Is your husband home, Melendie? I'm afraid it is urgent that we speak with him right away."

The light appeared to briefly leave Melendie's eyes, as though she knew her time with her family whole had come, once again, to an abrupt end. She forced a smile in spite of herself. "Of course. He's in the den. I'll show you in."

"Please," Malík added, knowing that she was feeling dismissed, "join us, won't you? And you too, Jono. I know this is your family's time together, and so I will not leave any decisions about that time to be made without your input."

Melendie lit up, but she kept her pleasure in check, as did Jono. It was not often that a warrior's wife and child were permitted to be a part of his business.

They entered the den to find Scarro seated in a chair, across a little table from his seventeen-year-old apprentice Ronan Kah.

Ronan slapped a choice card down on the table and crowed, "Take that, old man! You are beaten! Spanked!"

Scarro stood up straight and glowered down at the younger gnome, offering his most menacing look. "Mind your tongue, *apprentice*. There is such a thing as a sore winner."

"Warns the notoriously sore *loser*." Ronan only laughed more furiously.

Scarro's lip turned up at the corner, and he shook his head, offering no more levity than this, as he took his seat once more. "I am not a sore loser, Ronan. I learn from my defeats and give thanks for the lesson."

Ronan suddenly noticed that they were not alone and collected himself with a smile. "Scarro, we have company."

The warrior turned in his chair to look behind him, then stood apologetically. "Malík! I didn't know you were there. We were so into our game. To what do I owe the honor?" He noticed the shadowy countenance of the second shaman then and seemed almost taken aback. "Two shamans, I see. This house is doubly honored."

Malík waved away the flattery. "Nonsense, Scarro. I'm afraid we are here only to burden you and your family in your time of rest."

"Malík, this house is ever at your service. Was it not only a month ago that you cured Jono of the Boomflu? We are in your debt. Take a seat, both of you."

Jono cringed and avoided the shamans' glances at the mention of his previous illness.

"Boomflu?" Xersek asked Malík under his breath as they sat. "I've not heard of that."

"Yes, it's not common to your tribe, but we have yet to build immunities to the things that are in the air in this new territory."

"Ah. So what is it?"

Malík noted Jono's discomfort over the subject. "I'll spare you the details for now, old friend. Suffice it to say, Ak'ten would have found the illness … funny."

"Ah," Xersek got the picture, and he imagined countless messy baby garments to be cleaned. "Boom …"

When everyone was seated, Malík addressed the Jintos. "Well, my friends, I'm afraid we must get right to business."

He looked to the boy. "Jono, would you be so kind?" He held out Ak'ten, still cradled in is arms.

"Oh, yes!" Jono could not hide the fact that he thought Ak'ten, as a baby, was decidedly magical, all shamanistic qualities aside. He took the baby in his arms and studied him with wonder, giving him a finger to hold, while the shaman spoke.

"My fellow shaman, Xersek, has come to us with urgent need. It seems Tribe Riven has unearthed a terrible evil, and none from their own bloodlines can do anything to thwart it." He looked to Xersek.

"Yes," the younger shaman said. "I'll tell you what has happened." He looked to Jono with concern, then to the boy's father. "But I must warn you, Scarro, it may be too terrible for innocent ears to hear."

Scarro shook his head. "No. Jono will be a man soon. He will see terrible things in time and will likely die in battle some day, as all of our line from my great-great-grandfather Lorok to my father Kondo have done, and as surely I will do. The horrors of this world will be a part of my son's life then, so there is no reason to hide them from him now."

Melendie's eyes disagreed, as she studied her sweet son holding baby Ak'ten in his arms, but she said nothing.

"Very well," Xersek said, and he proceeded to tell Scarro, Melendie, Jono, and Ronan all that he had told Malík about the Demons of the Blood.

When Xersek had finished, everyone remained silent. The faces of Melendie and Jono registered sheer terror at the tale, while Ronan seemed more nervous than anything else, looking to his master for the proper emotional response. As for Scarro, the warrior stared into the fire of the hearth darkly. After a few long moments, he simply offered a contemplative, "Hmm."

"Will you help them, Father?" Jono asked tentatively. He and Ronan looked to the warrior with equal angst, both unsure of what they wanted him to say, both fairly certain what his answer would be.

Malík looked to Melendie. "We know this is a rare time for you all, with your family whole for only a short while. I cannot tell you enough how unhappy I am to have to ask for Scarro's aid at this time, but as you can see from Xersek's account, there isn't any time to wait. The later we put off the nightmare confrontation with this demon clan, the more powerful they will have become."

"I understand, Malík," Melendie replied. "I understood when I married him. My husband has dedicated his life to the protection of Tribe Qadash. He is free to fulfill that calling however he feels he must. I am very proud to be his wife."

Ronan spoke up then, not entirely sure about the whole thing. "Why do you need a warrior at all? I don't understand. Demons, spirits, dark magic ... These are a shaman's concerns alone, are they not?"

"Well—" Xersek began, only to be cut off by Scarro.

"Everything overlaps, Ronan," the warrior answered serenely, still staring into the fire. "If the threat is of great concern to shamans, then it is of great concern to us all. Malík has many times offered us aid on the battlefield, in matters of war, when he could have said that he only deals in medicine and matters of the spirit realm. Though you yourself fought valiantly during the horrors of Fenrir's Uprising last year, would any of us have survived without the aid of Malík? No. The matter at hand is for us *all* to solve." He looked to Malík. "We will join you. Ronan and I will help you to drive these Demons of the Blood from our world."

Malík noticed the effect these words had on the others. Xersek's face registered subtly with relief, while Melendie and Jono both looked sad, but resigned, and Ronan looked eager, if still a bit confused. "Thank you, Scarro," the shaman said. "Thank you, Melendie and Jono. I know what this means to all of you."

"My father is brave." Jono smiled proudly. "He *has* to go. It's a hero's quest, and he's a hero."

"Yes, yes," Ronan agreed sarcastically, having noticed that Malík had thanked all by name but him. "And I am only a shadow, not even worthy of thanks." He put a hand to his forehead in mock disappointment.

"Ronan!" Scarro barked.

The younger gnome laughed. " 'Tis a joke, old man! Just a joke." He nudged Jono with his elbow, and the younger boy laughed.

This disturbed Ak'ten's nap, and the baby woke, gurgling and grabbing a lock of Jono's long, black hair with the grip of merciless baby conquest.

"Ow!" Jono laughed, as Ak'ten pulled his head down. He tried to pry himself free, but Ak'ten would have none of it. The baby wailed with delight, then broke wind again and laughed out loud.

Jono and Ronan laughed as well, and Ronan helped to take the baby's relentless fist from Jono's hair, one pudgy finger at a time. "He likes you, Jono," Ronan said with amusement. "Perhaps he thinks you're his new mother. Go ahead." He nodded, then spoke in a more serious tone, "Try and feed him milk from your breast."

Both boys broke into boisterous laughter at this, and Ak'ten, feeling their merriment, squealed in happy accord.

"Enough, Jono," Scarro snapped, as he stood.

"But Ronan—"

"I said enough, boy." Scarro glared at him. "We must prepare to go to war now, perhaps to our deaths. You will do the same one day. This is a serious time."

"Yes, Father." Jono nodded his head, and Ak'ten began to whimper.

Melendie took Ak'ten then and soothed him back to quiet serenity.

"When do we leave?" Scarro asked Malík.

"Right away, I'm afraid," the shaman answered. "Xersek has an armadillo outside of the caverns awaiting us.

"Yes!" Ronan crowed. "We get to ride an armadillo! Those monsters are terrific!"

Jono lit up. "I've heard they are enormous!"

"They are that and more! They are born with armor, and they have giant claws! And they are so very huge that a score of warriors can ride one all at once!"

"Wow! I want to see it!"

"Another time, my son," Scarro said. He looked to his apprentice. "Ronan, go and get our things."

"Yes, Scarro."

As Ronan bounded off happily to obey his mentor, Jono pleaded with Scarro, "Father, please! I can help you carry your gear and load it on the armadillo, then I will come straight home. I promise!"

"It is dark, Son. There are many terrible things in the night that will make a quick meal of you. I cannot let you walk home alone."

"But the armadillo is just outside of the great tree, isn't it? You can see me back through the gates. I'll be safe. Please, Father! Please!"

Scarro smiled in spite of himself and put a hand on Jono's shoulder. "Very well, Son. Very well. Go and help Ronan with our gear."

"Thank you, Father! Thank you!"

Jono ran off to join Ronan, and Scarro shook his head. "Boys."

Malík laughed. "He has his father's courage and his mother's love of life. He is a good lad."

"He is indeed," Scarro agreed. "And one day soon, he will be dead, killed in battle, as all true warriors are; his blood poured out on some battlefield; remembered only by his children. He cannot be a merry boy much longer, I am afraid."

Xersek offered Malík a secret look that spoke volumes. It seemed Xersek was finally getting a taste of what he did to others with his own grim outlook, and even the demonologist found Scarro's perspective to be somewhat over the top with its severity.

Malík struggled not to giggle at the look upon his peer's bearded face. Rather than comment on Scarro's dark outlook on life, he turned his attention to Melendie. "My dear friend, might I ask one more favor of you before we depart?"

She smiled warmly. "Of course, Malík. What is it?"

"Ak'ten. Would you look after him while we're away? I can hardly leave him at home by himself after all."

"Of course!" Melendie lit up. "He's a sheer joy, Malík."

Malík grumbled. "Mind his sense of humor." He chuckled then and turned away, as Jono and Ronan returned, loaded down with weapons, food packs, canteens, and rolled up tents.

"We get to keep Ak'ten too?" Jono was elated. "Can he sleep in my room?"

"We'll see, Jono," Melendie answered, a laugh in her voice.

"Is that everything?" Scarro asked Ronan.

"Everything but the women and the wine." The apprentice nudged Jono again, and the younger boy snickered.

Melendie shook her head and rolled her eyes. "You boys have a merry adventure now, and come home to me in one piece. Both of you." She kissed Ronan on the forehead, then she kissed her husband tenderly on the lips.

Ak'ten suddenly found himself pressed between them, and he squealed with confusion at the two warm bodies on either side of him, all the more bewildered when they ignored his wordless utterances completely.

"We'll return to you victorious, Melendie, or we won't return at all," Scarro assured her.

She smirked. "I'd settle for the return of a defeated hero over no return at all."

Scarro kissed her again. "I love you. You are with me wherever I go. You know that, don't you?"

"Yes," she said. "And you with me. Forever and always."

Ronan spoke up then, "And I promise to return as well, Melendie. If not in one piece as you request, then, I vow, in no more than two."

Melendie laughed. "Get going, you foolish warriors. Go and save the day."

As they passed her on their way out the door, she patted her son on the head, loaded down as he was with the warriors' gear. "And you. Hurry home, my son. Don't be too eager for your father's way of life just yet."

"Yes, Mother." Jono laughed, as he wobbled out the door, struggling not to tip too far to one side or the other and lose his balance under the staggering weight of all that his father had given him to carry.

3
A Harsh Departure

The party of gnomes made their way back through the caverns and out through the main gates at the base of the great tree, Jono struggling to keep up. When at last they made it to the armadillo, Jono and Ronan put down their burdens, and Jono laughed at how wobbly his arms felt. Ronan, feeling the young boy's pain, could not help but join him in laughter, earning him a scowl from

Scarro, who wordlessly began loading their equipment into the carriage atop the mighty war beast.

Jono gazed up at the enormous creature with wonder. "Wow! It's such a monster! Can I pet it?"

Xersek laughed. "Of course you can, boy. But be careful not to startle him. Digger tends to jump when he's taken off guard."

Jono nodded and exchanged a look with Ronan. The two young gnomes grinned and scurried up to the creature, feeling its strange skin, gasping at the terrible size of its claws.

"What a beast," Ronan observed. "He certainly puts our tribe's squirrels to shame."

"Don't be so quick to judge, my friend," Xersek said. "Each animal has its strengths and weaknesses. Each is of equal value in our efforts against the Gremlins."

Ronan nodded, staring up at the massive, naturally armored behemoth called Digger.

"Ronan," Scarro snapped. "Help with the equipment."

"Yes, Scarro." Ronan scampered off to help his mentor load their supplies, as Malík and Xersek were already doing. He looked back. "Come on, Jono. Grab some of our gear and bring it up, so you can see the carriage."

Jono eagerly bounced after his father's apprentice, doing just that. The climb with a full load of equipment was tricky, up the rope ladder that hung down the creature's side from the covered carriage strapped onto its back. When Jono got to the top, he followed Ronan's lead, packing the supplies he'd carried into compartments on the inside of the carriage. He wasted no time thereafter in running to the side of the carriage and looking over, seeing his father and the two shamans conversing so far below them. It seemed so much higher from this vantage point than it had from the ground. He studied the carriage itself, the poles that held the decorative, protective tarp above. There were curtains tied off to the sides all around that could be closed to keep out the weather. Cushioned seats with pillows surrounded the inside of the carriage. "I could *live* here!"

Ronan laughed. "On the back of a beast? I think you'd tire of it quickly, Jono."

"No." Jono shook his head, sincere. "This is so much better than my room. No wonder Tribe Riven has tamed these armadillos. Who could ever get at their warriors here?"

Ronan still smiled, but there was a sadness in his eyes. "You'd be surprised. No one is ever safe in a war. Especially if they think they're invincible."

"Now you sound like my father."

Ronan smirked. "Well, he has been my master for the past five years. Bound to rub off some, here and there. But I still know how to have fun."

It was now Jono's turn to look sad. "My father never has fun. He never laughs. He is always so … hopeless."

"Aw, he's not hopeless. He's just prepared. He may dwell on the darker side of possibilities before a battle, but he's always ready. He always has a plan, because he knows what's out there. He knows all the worst that could happen."

"But there's no plan now, is there?" Jono asked, worried. "These demon things, they haven't been faced for thousands of years."

"Well," Ronan assured him smugly. "I have a plan."

"You do?" Jono lit up. "What sort of plan?"

"If those demons jump up in this carriage, for one, I'll know just what to do."

"What's that?"

"This!" Ronan put two fingers at the sides of his mouth and another two into his nostrils and pulled his face into a hideous form, sticking out his tongue and warbling at Jono.

Jono laughed out loud and fell back into one of the cushioned seats. "That's it, Ronan! The demons will fall before you in droves! I can fight them too!" Jono made his own strange, tongue-wagging face and peculiar vocalizations, causing Ronan to laugh just as hard. The boys continued to trade faces and hearty laughter, until the stern voice of Scarro cut them off.

"*What* are you boys doing?"

Ronan immediately straightened up and stood to attention.

Jono, having not picked up on the anger in his father's voice, turned and answered, "This!" making his strangest face yet, lolling his tongue, crossing his eyes, and uttering sheer nonsense at the seasoned warrior.

"*Jono*!" Scarro glared down at his son and raised a hand, as if to strike him.

Jono jumped back and stood to attention beside Ronan, his eyes beginning to water as if his father had actually landed the threatened blow. "I'm sorry, Father! We were just—"

"You were *just* …" Scarro lowered his hand, regretting the gesture. He spoke in a calmer voice, though no less stern. "You were just fooling around. And only fools *play* the fool at times such as these. Jono, my son, need I remind you again? In just two years' time, Ronan will be a warrior, a man, and you will begin your time as an apprentice. You will enter into a world of pain, suffering, and death. You will see your friends die as well as your enemies. You will draw blood, and others will draw your blood. Likely you will see *me* die in battle, as my father died in battle, and his father before him. It is the lot of a warrior, and it is for the protection of the tribe. It is not a thing to be taken lightly. There is *no* room for laughter, on or off of the battlefield, if you are to last five minutes as a warrior."

Jono looked down, hiding his silent tears of shame. "I'm sorry, Father."

Scarro softened, pulling his son to him and hugging him. "You are learning, Jono." He put a hand on the boy's shoulder and held him at arm's length, meeting his eyes. "I only want what's best for you. Now, run along home. You'll be the man of the house while I'm away. Your mother will be depending on you."

The two shamans climbed into the carriage then with the last of the supplies, having listened to the entire exchange from the ladder.

Jono nodded to his father and went to the ladder himself, before turning back. "Father?"

"Yes, Jono?"

"Must *all* warriors die in such a way?"

"Yes."

"But what about the old men in the taverns?"

Scarro shook his head. "That is no life, my son. A true warrior never grows old. He never has the chance."

"But—"

"Son, I am not telling you these things to be cruel. I am telling you so that you will be prepared. Any time I leave for battle, it may be the last time we see one another. Tonight may be our last goodbye. I want you to know it. I want you to be ready. I want you to be strong. Even Ronan may die in battle before he is a warrior in full. This will be your life one day, and you will never do well if you are always laughing and making a joke of war. Now, if this *is* our last goodbye, live a good life. Take care of your mother. And die a warrior's death."

Jono turned and began to climb down the ladder, disheartened. Then he smiled again and said, "Father, I do not wish you a warrior's death. I wish you to be wrong in all that you have said."

Bewildered, Scarro asked, "Why, son? Why would you offer me such insult when we may never see each other again?"

"Because we *will* see each other again." Jono smiled brightly, though tears remained in his eyes. "Because … you *always* come home." The boy hurried down the ladder and scampered back to the main gates, eager to have the last word on the matter.

As Xersek rolled up the rope ladder and pulled it into the carriage, Scarro watched his son, as the guards let him back into the caverns of their tribe and into the safety of the world Scarro knew he would one day die to protect. "Goodbye, Son," he spoke quietly, for no one's ears but his own. "May we both die well."

Ronan flopped down onto the cushions of the carriage seats. "Well, you certainly did lay it on thick, old man." He laughed. "Again."

"Remember your place, apprentice," Scarro said softly.

"I'm just saying, the way Jono says goodbye to his father and the way I say goodbye to mine are very different. My father the baker! He always says, 'Be safe, my son! I shall have your favorite blueberry pie waiting on you when you return.' And so, I always leave hungry and dreaming of blueberry pie.

"Jono's father says, 'Goodbye, Son. I shall surely die, and you shall too.' And poor Jono goes home dreaming of death and becoming as grim as his father some day." He laughed. "I much prefer the blueberries." He sighed, dreamily. "The blueberries of life."

"Too many berries will make you sick, Ronan. My son will be stronger for knowing what's to come on the day that it finally does."

"Yes, well," Xersek interrupted. "Everyone have a seat. There's always a bit of a lurch when Digger starts off, and it's time we got on our way." He exchanged a look with Malík, shaking his head at Scarro's disposition.

Malík shrugged, as he and Scarro took their seats. "We really have lucked out, Xersek. Scarro has seen many battles, as you can surely tell. Perhaps I shall regale you with the tales of some of his more notable exploits as we travel."

Xersek took the reins in his hands. "Oh, I should love to hear them. From *you*." He pulled the reigns. "Onward, Digger! Into the forest!"

As promised, the entire carriage lurched, and Ronan rolled right off of his cushions and onto the floor. He laughed at himself and struggled back into his seat against the rocking of the creature's movement, holding himself in place by gripping the outside of the carriage with both arms. "So how do we know where we're going, anyway? Did not the Demons of the Blood flee into parts unknown?"

"Indeed," Xersek said. "But my staff will lead us to them. I fashioned it with the legendary Demon Stone."

"Some legend," Ronan replied sarcastically. "Never heard of it." He noticed that Digger seemed to be turning slowly in a circle. "What—?"

"Oh, you may not have heard of it, young apprentice," Xersek said, "but you will surely *tell* of it after this adventure." As the armadillo continued to turn, the pitch black stone in Xersek's staff shifted color, into a deep purple, and began to glow until it shined quite brightly. "That's it, Digger." He pulled the reigns, stopping Digger's turning. "That's the way we must go."

The armadillo began going forward, and Xersek laid his staff on the floor beside him, hiding its glow from any eyes that might have been looking upon them from outside of the carriage. "The Demon Stone can track demons, and it can fell them. This staff and I have witnessed many horrible things." A look of haunted satisfaction crossed the demonologist's face. "Yes … terrible things. It will lead us to *these* monsters as well."

Malík noticed the look of exasperation on Ronan's face; a look that was silently begging the fates for no more grim words this night. Malík smiled at Ronan. "Care to play cards?"

"Yes!" Ronan reached into a pocket on his belt and pulled out a deck that he immediately began to shuffle, a grin of gratitude and relief all but glowing from his face. "Get ready to lose, shaman!"

Malík laughed. "Somehow, I knew you'd be up for a game." He winked.

Ronan dealt the cards with a decidedly thankful nod.

4
Of Fathers, Sons, and Scars

Digger carried them for hours into the forest, the Demon Stone leading them strongly at times, then glowing not at all.

After losing three games to the young warrior's apprentice, Malík called it a night and went to sit beside his old friend in the driver's seat. He studied the darkness all around them with a weary sigh, his ears ever alert for the many dangers the deep forest held, not only from the predatory creatures of the night, but from the human world that surrounded the forest on all sides with its infernal technology.

As if to illustrate his fears, his eyes caught the glint of a broken bottle in the brush, surrounded by various other bits of human litter, each far larger than any gnome Malík had ever known. He considered that the greatest danger of the human world was its indifference; its clumsiness. Humans threw things into the wood without any regard for the smaller creatures living there; creatures like gnomes who would be crushed by the massive "baseballs" and other toys the humans were wont to toss into the woods on a whim. It was bad enough that their bedeviled technological advancements had caused them to erect the myriad street lights and porch lights that had erased most of the stars from the night sky.

Malík sat back, remembering the stars that used to fill the darkness, countless and comforting; a reminder that there were always greater things out there, at any given moment, than what one shaman ever faced in a lifetime. Far greater even than the worst of any of those things. He thought of his lost apprentice.

Xersek noted the look of sad introspection on his friend's bearded face. "What troubles you, Malík?"

"The peaceful quiet of nights like this I'm afraid."

"Really? I don't follow."

"The past year has been a terror," Malík stated solemnly. "And now, with Ak'ten to tend to, there is seldom a moment's peace to be had. When the peace comes, the memories flood in. The reality of what I've been through. The regrets." He looked down, tears in his eyes. "I failed Fenrir, Xersek. I failed him as a teacher, and I fear that I will fail Ak'ten in the same way."

Xersek patted his old friend on the shoulder reassuringly. "No, Malík. You mustn't do that to yourself. What Fenrir did, rising up against his own, using his magical gifts and all that you had taught him to destroy Tribe Qadash, falling in with the Darkgnomes; that was all his own choice. It was his *nature* that failed him, Malík, not you."

"I wish it were easy for me to think so, my friend. The truth is, he was nothing like other shamans' apprentices. He was from the royal clan, a warrior and a Centenarian, in spite of our rules against it. He was the exception to *every* rule, because he fought to be. I tried to teach him like any other apprentice, but I think all he wanted in life was not to be controlled by anyone. I may have pushed him too hard to make a choice. I may have wounded him and made him run all the harder from the shaman's life by making him feel trapped." He shook his head. "It all comes back to me, on quiet nights like this. I can't stop myself from pondering what might have been, had I done things differently."

Xersek nodded. "Would it help if I reminded you that this is not at all a peaceful night? We are searching for an ancient demonic foe that bathes in blood, a kidnapped child, and the quiet night around us in these woods is filled with hungry arachnids, wild Moon Witches, and soul-sucking wraiths that blend in with the shadows themselves."

"You certainly have … perspective, Xersek."

Scarro, who had been listening quietly to the exchange, broke into the conversation, "Malík, no one in the tribe holds you to blame for Fenrir. He was a warrior as well as a shaman's apprentice, as you said. I served with him. He was troubled from the start. He had many victories, but he was never a hero. And you shamans begin training your apprentices from infancy. You are their fathers in this way. It is your duty to push your sons to make choices, to become something rather than nothing. And if we do our part, Malík, we *will* hurt them. We will *scar* our sons and daughters. The trick is making sure they get all the *right* scars."

"Perhaps we are no longer speaking of Fenrir, hmm, Scarro?" Malík smiled weakly. "Is that why you are so harsh with Jono? Are you trying to give him the *right* scars?"

"I am," Scarro agreed without hesitation. "He's a Jinto, from the line of Lorok. He must be prepared for the life, and the death, that awaits him."

"But do you always depart from him on these grim terms?" Malík asked. "Surely it wouldn't hurt to give the boy *some* hope." He looked to Ronan, who had fallen asleep on the cushions. "Perhaps he'd rather be left thinking of blueberry pie, as Ronan does."

"Ronan …" Scarro shook his head. "Jono is not Ronan. And my father left me with similar words, every time he went into battle, just as his father did with him, and his father before him, and all spoke true.

"I remember the day my father died. I was like Jono. I was carefree. I hadn't believed him, because he'd promised so often never to return. Then when he was killed, during the Diamond War, I knew he had done all that he could to prepare me. I accepted that he had been honest with me all along. I became the son he had hoped I would be, and never again doubted the things he had told me about my life and death to come. I grew a warrior's heart right then and there, at the age of nine, younger than Jono is now. Our line has produced five celebrated warriors, from Lorok to myself, because we are tempered by our fathers at an early age. We leave boyhood and frivolity behind, and we never expect a long life to be our reward."

"Yes," Malík said. "You know, I knew Lorok, and his son, Tomar, and Tomar's son, Pall'dan, and Pall'dan's son Kondo, just as I now know Kondo's son Scarro, and Scarro's son Jono. All of them such naturally happy children. And what you may not realize is that Lorok, your great-great-grandfather, upon his dying breath, wanted nothing more than for Tomar to live a life of joy and prosperity. A long life.

"And when Tomar died, having forced himself to be so severe for so long, he regretted nothing more than having taught his own son to do the same, but my own words to their sons were spoken upon deaf ears both times. They felt that in order to honor their fathers, they must abhor all whimsy." He smiled. "I still remember the day I went to your father and mother, to tell them you had the magic; to tell them that, if they chose it for you, you could be trained as a shaman and live for a thousand years healing some other great tribe. How angry Kondo was that anyone should seek to disillusion his son with such nonsense."

Scarro laughed, and he spoke carefully, "Perhaps your own centuries of such a life have confused you, old shaman. It was not Kondo who you had this conversation with, but me and Melendie, about Jono. Don't you remember? It was less than ten years ago."

"Ah, yes, we three *did* have that conversation, but that was more than a quarter of a century later, and your words were almost identical to your father's. No mistake at all."

"But, Malík …" Scarro paused, stunned at the revelation. "Are you certain?"

Xersek broke in, "Oh, yes. He is certain, child. I remember when you turned him down for Jono, and how he said it had been just as it was with your father before you."

"And of course, your patriarch, Methule, forbade me ever to tell you," Malík added.

"But you just *did* tell me!"

"So I did." Malík shrugged. "I'm old. I must have forgotten momentarily that I wasn't supposed to." He looked subtly to Xersek, who chuckled under his breath. "But I digress. I only meant to illustrate that the first gnome in this line of warriors from which you hail, all of whom died so nobly in battle, did not want his descendants to be so afraid of living a life filled with hopes, with dreams. With possibilities."

He studied Scarro's bewildered face, satisfied that he'd gotten the callused gnome of the sword thinking. "So tell me, why do you tolerate so much more from your apprentice than you do from your son? Surely, if any should be learning not to have hope for a long life as a warrior, it should be your apprentice."

"Ronan's different," Scarro said matter-of-factly. "He does his own thing. Normally that would be problematic, but it seems to work for him exceedingly well. It's almost a joke that he's still an apprentice for two years to come. You know, he was given a magical sword, Firebolt, by the king of Tribe Sempiira, for saving his daughter."

"A magical sword, within *our* caverns, and *I* didn't know about it? You never thought it *might* be wise to tell me?"

"Forgive me, Malík. It seemed a trifle. It is just another weapon really, but I forbid him—"

"It shoots energy bolts, if I will it to!" Ronan sat up happily from where he'd lain. "Want me to show you?"

"Energy bolts?" Malík said, outwardly incensed, while secretly amused. "Yes, Ronan, I think that you must, but … some other time. We wouldn't want to draw attention from … Moon Witches … or something of that sort."

"Malík doesn't care for Moon Witches," Xersek offered, a teasing tone in his voice. "Finds them threatening. One in particular—"

Malík cleared his throat abruptly. "Yes, well …"

"As I was saying," said Scarro, "I forbid him to use the sword's magical properties, except under certain conditions. I feel it takes away from his training. He shouldn't be relying on magic swords, when he might not always have one. Besides, it makes the other apprentices jealous. But he did earn it. Doing his own thing, as I say, has always worked for him. So I'm more lenient with him than I might otherwise be. He's proven himself, time and again."

"That's *right* I have," beamed the apprentice. "Stick around, Scarro. Someday I'll teach you all that I know."

Scarro grumbled. "I thought you were sleeping only moments ago! Was this some ruse to listen in on our conversation?"

Xersek chuckled. "Youngsters are always awake when they are asleep, when their elders are having secret conversations in the dark."

"Let me see that sword, Ronan," Malík said, curiosity getting the better of him.

'Sure thing, Malík!" Ronan went to his equipment bag and removed a sword in its scabbard, carrying it over to the shaman of his tribe.

Malík took the sheath and pulled out the glistening sword, letting out an involuntary moan of wonder. "What a magnificent blade!" He held it up and gave it a proper once over. "And you say it shoots 'energy bolts?' "

"It does. Too bad Scarro won't let me wield it in battle. Otherwise you could see."

"Indeed." Malík returned the sword to its sheath and handed it back to the youth. "Tribe Sempiira, eh? They have some very old magic in those caverns. That's quite a gift."

Ronan smiled proudly.

"I wonder," Malík mused aloud, "how Jono would fare, if he were encouraged to do his 'own thing' as well."

Scarro was about to reply, when the other shaman cut him off.

"Whoah!" Xersek barked, looking to the staff at his feet. "We're getting close. The stone is glowing hot in this direction. I think we're almost upon them. Better get ready."

Scarro and Ronan went immediately into battle mode, securing their weapons of choice and preparing for the ordeal to come.

5
Caverns of the Lost Tribe

When at last Xersek brought Digger to a stop, the group had arrived at a rocky hill, surrounded by trees. The gnomes made their way down the rope ladder, and Xersek took a special rope with him and immediately set to work tying the armadillo to the nearest tree.

"Won't that leave him vulnerable to predation?" Ronan asked.

"I'm a shaman, boy," Xersek said. "And this is a magic rope."

Ronan laughed. "Magic how? Does it do battle with wolves and coyotes on its own?"

"Don't be silly," Xersek huffed.

Ronan shrugged. "Well, you said it was magic. How should I know what sort of magic is silly or not?"

As Xersek tied the knots, he patiently explained. "It's a cloak of sorts. It prevents predators from even seeing him, just as it prevents him from seeing them and running off."

"What if one of the humans' steeds comes down here? The ones that are made of metal, with lights for eyes, that are always killing smaller animals?" Ronan asked.

"They won't. Those monstrosities never leave the rivers of rock. Digger will be quite safe down here."

Malík assessed their location. "This *must* be the place. I can feel it. These rocks are … haunted." He tapped his staff on the ground, and the green stone at its top lit up, changing color, from green to deep red, as the magic of the shaman was channeled through it.

Scarro spoke sternly to his apprentice, "Ronan, is that Firebolt strapped to your back?"

"It is. I brought her just in case you decided I need her."

"You won't," the warrior said. "And I won't. You have a perfectly good normal sword right there in your hand."

Ronan shrugged. "Like I said. Just in case."

Scarro shook his head, letting the matter go.

"So," Ronan asked him. "You could have been a shaman. Is that why you can see ghosts?"

Both shamans looked to Scarro, who grumbled. "That's no one's concern."

"But you might have been a shaman, if your father had allowed it. I just wondered—"

"Enough, Ronan," Scarro snapped. "Besides, I haven't really had time to weigh the hows and whys of my abilities against this new information. I only *just* found out that I might have been a shaman."

"Ah!" Xersek called. "Oh … my. Malík, can you read these glyphs?" He held his staff to the rocky hillside, shining purple light on some very old writing that he'd found carved there.

Malík approached, adding his own staff's soft crimson glow. "Xersek … this is extraordinary."

"What is it?" Scarro asked.

"Well," Xersek answered, "considering the glyphs are from a form neither Malík nor I are familiar with, there are a *few* possibilities. But, I think," he shined his light closer, revealing a subtle entrance to the rocky wall itself, cloaked in shadows, "we may have stumbled upon the caverns of the Lost Tribe."

"The Lost Tribe?" Ronan asked.

"Yes," Malík said. "Many adventurers have spoken of such a ruin. And the antiquity of these glyphs at the entrance, the lack of any guards, the fact that we know of no gnome tribe living in this area, all point to this being the location of the mysterious caverns that were abandoned, it is thought, ten thousand years ago, by either gnomes or very gnome-like beings. The identity of this ancient tribe, and the reason for their disappearance, are entirely unknown."

Xersek looked over the party of gnomes who had followed him on this quest, sizing them up one last time before they crossed the point of no return. "Yes. A ghost cavern, so to speak." He nodded gravely, then said, in a hauntingly cold almost-whisper, "Let's go in."

Xersek led the way, with the glowing purple light of his staff, and the gnomes from Tribe Qadash followed him into the darkness.

6
In the Demons' Lair

The gnomes walked ever farther into the darkness of the mysterious caverns, lighted only by the glowing staves of the shamans. The carvings and glyphs along the walls were alien things, unreadable, unrelatable. Malík mumbled to Xersek quietly, "Are you sure about just … walking in?"

"It was an inevitability, Malík," Xersek answered, "one way or another. The monsters would not have come out to us. They want us in their comfort zone. They want to be sure that they have the upper hand in knowing the layout of this place, while all we are capable of is stumbling around in the dark."

"So," Scarro put in, having overheard, "again, the wisdom in this move?"

"As I said," Xersek answered, "inevitability. Might as well get started now as wait an hour to figure out the only way to get where we're going is to play the demons' game. But only so far."

Suddenly, the room lit up, torches along the walls blazing to life, and Ronan screamed.

"Ronan!" Scarro called out, his eyes struggling to adjust to the light.

As Scarro approached, Ronan was clutching his chest, not sure whether to scream again or not. The reality of what was before him was slowly sinking in, in spite of his initial terror.

"Just a statue, Ronan." Scarro patted his apprentice on the back. "Relax."

Ronan caught his breath, looking back at the monstrous black and red sculpture, baring its fangs, with nine wild eyes and six ferocious horns. "I almost wet myself. It is a hideous statue."

"Yes," Xersek agreed. "It appears to be some sort of deity. A guardian perhaps? It's a common belief that monstrous statues can keep evil spirits at bay."

Malík harrumphed, wholly skeptical of such a simplistic notion. "So we were taught as apprentices. But I've never seen such things put to the test. You're the expert, Xersek. Is there any truth to that old lore?"

Xersek, looking now right past Malík, answered in his unnerving almost-whisper, that Malík knew well to precede dread revelations, "See for yourself."

The gnomes all turned to follow Xersek's gaze, and they saw a gnome in rich but tattered garments, his hair disheveled, his eyes and ears bleeding, standing in the archway leading into another corridor. His voice was ghastly, harsh, ungnomelike, raspy as though it was an excruciating thing to use his vocal cords at all, "I'd say not … *not.*"

"Bin Riven!" Scarro realized aloud. "What have they done to you?"

"They… *they*?" The bleeding eyes of the purloined body before him turned their terrifying gaze on Scarro. "There is no they, foolish meat creature … *creature*. I am the Demons of the Blood … *blood*."

"Who is he, really?" Ronan asked Scarro. "And why is he talking like that?"

"He's a prince of Clan Riven. A first cousin to King Soma, and a friend. I don't know why he's talking like that, except that—"

"Except that it isn't him," Xersek interjected. "This is a lackey of the Demons of the Blood, and he is talking like that, because he is insane, as are all beings of pure evil."

The thing with Bin Riven's body laughed, and the rasping, grating sound of it was like the very chill of death itself. "Yes. We are insane … *insane*. Now, where is the crown prince? Have you brought us the prince as promised … *promised*?"

Xersek gripped his staff tighter, and Malík, noting the subtle move, followed suit, ready for battle.

"No," Xersek answered the demon. "We have not brought Prince Infractus. We have come to negotiate for Prince Lumino's return to his father and the departure of your demon clan from these bodies."

The demon laughed again, and the horrifying sound of cackling death required all of Ronan's will not to put his hands up to his ears and weep. In fact, his hands were beginning to sweat, even as he gripped his sword. He looked to Scarro, who seemed sad, but resigned. Not a trace of fear was visible within the hardened warrior's countenance. Ronan made an effort to suppress his own fear, to be like Scarro.

Suddenly, the demon snapped out of its laughter and bit out with an unabashed rage, "There will be no negotiation! … *negotiation.* Terms of the surrender of Tribe Riven are absolute … *absolute.*" He grinned, thirstily, wiping some of the blood from his ears and licking his fingers. "You will all die … *die.*"

Scarro moved then like lightning, accosting the demon and pinning him to the wall, the heroic warrior's sword to his throat. "I am no shaman or exorcist, but you have robbed my friend of his body, and I *demand* you return it to him at once!"

Again, the horrible, cackling laughter.

Before he knew what was happening, Scarro found himself flying backwards and crashing into the opposite wall, pinned and unable to move, held by invisible hands. With a struggle, he uttered in defiance, "Monster … I do not fear you."

Ronan, wasting no time at all, threw his sword with deadly aim at the demon's stolen face, but a blast of mystic light from Xersek's staff knocked the blade off course. "No!" The shaman said. "I remind you, Ronan, we are here to *rescue* Clan Riven, not to destroy it. Before you is an innocent gnome who can still have his body returned to him."

Ronan looked away. "I'm sorry, I—"

"Sorry!" Mocked the demon with a malicious sneer. "… *Sorry*." He projected a fountain of blood from his mouth in Ronan's direction, but the young gnome deftly dodged the morbid assault.

While the demon was distracted, Xersek shined an intense light from the Demon Stone onto the body of Bin Riven. "By the power of the Demon Stone, I command you, *leave* this body! Leave the body of Prince Bin Riven *at once*!"

The demon, though now writhing in anguish on the ground, still managed a cackling laugh. "At once … *once*."

The body of the prince went still.

Xersek looked to the air before him and shot out another blast of mystic light from the Demon Stone at the now disembodied demon in their midst. "Malík, help me!"

Malík instantly channeled his own magical willpower into his staff, and a soft crimson glow joined the light from Xersek's weapon, holding the demon where it was.

The demon writhed and screamed, as Xersek removed from the deep pocket inside his robe a strange little lantern. Keeping one hand firmly on his staff, he called to the warrior's apprentice, "Ronan, quickly! Come and open the hatch!"

Not knowing what was going on at all, or what he was doing, Ronan ran to do as the shaman had instructed. He easily identified the little door at the front of the lantern and opened it up, then jumped back, as the demon roared out in defiance, and the lantern sucked it in violently.

When the ordeal was over, Xersek snapped the hatch closed on the lantern, and the demon bounced around within it, trying to break the glass, to no avail.

"What is *that*?" Ronan asked of the lantern.

"It is a necessary tool. We've no time for explanations, other than that it will hold as many demons as we can stuff into it. I've place a very powerful magic over the little trap."

"Well then," Malík said. "We've gotten the obligatory request for negotiations out of the way. How do you want to proceed?"

Xersek considered, placing the lantern back into his pocket. He looked to the gem at the top of his staff, glowing intensely and pointing the way. He looked down to Prince Bin. "First, we must get our young prince out of these caverns."

He knelt down to try and rouse the prince, shaking him. When the prince did not respond, he put a finger to the gnome's neck, then his wrist. He looked up, the blood having run from his face, to meet Malík's eyes.

"No …" Malík knelt down to verify it for himself.

"What happened?" Ronan asked, as he retrieved his sword. "What's wrong?"

"He's died, hasn't he, Xersek?" Scarro asked stoically.

Xersek nodded somberly. "Yes. He has left us."

As the two shamans stood, Malík offered, "I'm so sorry, Xersek. There was nothing you could have done. He must have been dead a while before we even encountered him here."

"How can that be?" Ronan asked, horrified.

Xersek explained, still in shock himself. "It is rare, but there are occasions when the possessed body is so damaged by the demon within it that the body cannot live after the demon has departed. It is a terrible end to such an ordeal. We defeat the demon, but we do not win."

"It is the call of Nubus," Scarro said, a sadness in his voice at the loss of his friend Bin. "We all must answer before too long." He knelt down and closed the bloody eyes of the fallen prince. "Rest well, as you died well, friend Bin."

"So what do we do now?" Ronan asked. "How many gnomes have these things possessed?"

"One hundred thirty-five more," Xersek answered. "And don't worry, young Ronan. I assure you that a death such as this is exceedingly rare." He looked to Scarro. "While we must still try to rescue the possessed, be ever ready. If it comes to battle, we will need your warrior skills. Malík and I are not soldiers. Though we can hold our own in a magical battle, this battle is only half magical. The rest is flesh and bone." He nodded to the mysterious stone that had led them this far. "Now, we go forward, into the viper's nest."

As they followed Xersek from the room, where lay the body of Bin Riven, Scarro moved next to his apprentice and quietly said, "Ronan, I feel you may do well to bring Firebolt into this battle."

"I'm way ahead of you, old man." Ronan dropped his normal sword to the ground right then and there, and he unsheathed Firebolt from where it had been strapped upon his back.

7
Four Against Legion

As the party of would-be heroes continued down the corridors, the torches on the wall continued to light up magically to usher them on.

"Okay," Ronan finally asked, "which one of you is doing that?"

"Neither, I'm afraid," Malík answered. "It's safe to assume our enemies are urging us on."

"That's comforting," Ronan muttered sarcastically.

"Not particularly," Xersek countered, wholly indifferent to Ronan's mordant tone.

The corridor ended, and they walked into a great chamber. The torches and candles throughout the enormous room burst into light, and the gnomes took in the horrific sight of the Demons of the Blood who occupied it.

Scarro showed no emotion, as he scanned the room, taking in the horrible faces of the possessed gnomes, instinctively searching for weaknesses within their ranks. It was difficult to make out any identifying features on the monsters' faces, as the sea of demons parted to allow them to continue forward, covered in blood from the eyes as they were. Scarro's stomach threatened to betray his horror, but he suppressed it, breathing in deeply, gripping the handle of his sword ever tighter, as it rested in the scabbard at his side.

The four gnomes marched bravely forward, following Xersek's lead, the demons parting before them until they found their way nearer to the front of the chamber.

"How much longer are we going to walk into this?" Ronan whispered to Scarro.

"Shh," was his teacher's sharp reply.

Suddenly, Xersek stopped, and he stamped his staff on the ground, a loud thunderclap sounding magically throughout the chamber. "I am Xersek the exorcist, and I demand an audience with the six unholy chiefs of the Demons of the Blood!"

Rasping laughter filled the room, and even powerful Malík felt his nerves begin to give, though he had long since learned to trust his friend Xersek's knowledge in such matters as these.

More demons parted, and a dais became visible at the very front of the room, at the center of which rested a throne, surrounded by six decaying corpses. A frightened child sat in the throne itself, bound and gagged. His wide, terrified eyes looked to the group of heroes pleadingly. Though barely three years of age, the child's terror did not result in tears.

Malík knew his words were not necessary, but he felt it would not hurt to offer comfort all the same. "Be brave, Prince Lumino. We've come to save you."

A smile of hope flashed through the child's expressive eyes, and Malík was satisfied, all the more determined to rescue the child and be done with this terrible adventure.

One of the corpses moved forward and spoke in a voice that made clear his throat was not entirely intact, "We are the chiefs, and you are the meat and the blood, the bread and the wine … *wine*. You have not brought Prince Infractus? … *Infractus*?"

"No," Xersek said boldly. "We have an alternative proposal."

"We do not seek alternatives … *alternatives*."

The one hundred twenty-nine lesser demons began closing in around the little rescue party.

"Yes," Xersek said, "I thought as much, however; I must say, I really don't care. You have taken the body of King Thanatos, I see. Possessed corpses are useless to me," this he spoke for the benefit of the warriors. "There is nothing left of the spirit that they once housed either to save or appeal to. So … here is my alternate proposal."

Xersek raised up his staff and slammed it back down onto the ground, a wave of purple light knocking the surrounding demons back, against their will.

Malík looked to Scarro and Ronan. "Save the prince. We'll handle the rest."

The warrior and his apprentice nodded and rushed to the dais.

As the possessed gnomes regained their feet and began closing back in, Malík and Xersek fought them off with the power channeled through their staves. Malík, not quite the expert exorcist as Xersek, was unable to exorcise the demons without the aid of a ritual, but he did have the power to force the demons back as they came at him or went after Scarro and Ronan.

Xersek, on the other hand, had the Demon Stone upon his staff. "In the name of the Demon Stone, I command you to leave these bodies *at once*!" Another great wave shot forth from his staff, and suddenly thirty demons were severed from their unwilling host bodies, flying through the air.

Malík gave his full attention to helping Xersek to capture them and put them in the lantern, one by one, before they could return to their stolen bodies.

As the shamans battled the demons behind them, Scarro and Ronan found themselves on either side of the throne, the child bouncing excitedly in his seat, eager to be released from his bonds.

Scarro lopped the head off of one of the chiefs whose body was little more than rotten skin over bone, pushing the thing backwards with his boot. "Ronan, grab the prince!"

The apprentice reached for little Lumino, but the child was snatched up by the chief who had taken the body of the late King Thanatos.

The demon chief levitated into the air and cackled awfully. "You will not have this tot until we have his father and all of Tribe Riven … *Riven.*"

The other chiefs had stopped pursuing the warriors, standing back to watch instead. The body Scarro had decapitated simply picked up its severed head and held it upon its neck, laughing.

Scarro took a dagger from his belt, without hesitation, and threw it with deadly aim at the levitating chief. He was surprised when the knife stopped in mid-air, turned, and shot straight back towards him. Though he used all of his speed to dodge the blade, it still managed to graze his arm on the way to the stone floor. As it hit the ground, Scarro looked up to see the other chiefs hungrily regarding his fresh wound.

The levitating chief, blood pouring forth from the necrotic sockets of his eyes, grinned terribly at Scarro. "You have lost, warrior … *warrior.* Surrender now, and we will make quick sport of you. None of your weapons can harm us … *us.*"

"Oh, yeah?" Ronan taunted, pointing Firebolt in the direction of the demon's face. "What do you say to this?"

Just as the demon chief began laughing anew at what he saw as a pitiful attempt at bravado, ten energy bolts flew forth from the tip of the gnome's sword and blew his head right off of his neck. Stunned, the demon dropped little Lumino.

Scarro's response was instantaneous, as he leapt forward and caught the falling toddler in his arms, rewarding Ronan with a subtle smile and a nod of approval that warmed the apprentice's heart with pride.

When Scarro removed the ropes and the gag from the child, Lumio pointed angrily over the warrior's shoulder to where the possessed body of King Thanatos was picking up its lost head. The child's eyes narrowed, and he vowed to the bewildered demon chief, "I go wee-wee on your mouf!"

He looked around the room. "I go wee-wee on *all* your moufs!"

The possessed Thanatos tried to return his head to its proper place, only to find that the energy bolt had destroyed any chance of this body ever being whole again. He rolled his bleeding eyes as well as he could in annoyance.

"Ronan," Scarro said. "End him."

Ronan's eyes narrowed, as he grinned his acquiescence. He let loose a steady stream of energy bolts from Firebolt, right into the body of King Thanatos, until the entire cadaver had been reduced to nothing more than a smoking pile of flesh and bone.

The now bodiless demon chief took to the air, and was in little time caught in the light of Malík's staff, ushering him towards Xersek's lantern.

"Leave just one of them intact, lads," Malík ordered them urgently. "Xersek says it is imperative."

"Pick one," Scarro said to Ronan.

"That one." Ronan pointed to the other headless chief, whose skull was wobbling around pathetically on his neck.

"Good choice. The rest die." Scarro moved on the chosen chief, who was having a hard time seeing, and knocked his head right back off with a well placed kick, then kicked the head across the floor, sending the body chasing after it. He grabbed a torch from the wall and lit the closest corpse demon on fire, while Ronan went on to blast two more with Firebolt.

"Where's the sixth one?" Scarro asked.

Ronan shrugged.

"He'll turn up. Walking corpses aren't exactly discreet." Scarro set down Prince Lumino. "Take Lumino out of here, to safety. Find a defensible position in the corridor outside. I'll find the last chief. There's little else we can do. Only the shamans can help the living victims."

Ronan nodded, and Lumino trotted over to him eagerly, to be picked up in his arms. As the other demons were distracted by the threat of the shamans, Ronan made his way around them, quietly sneaking towards the exit with the child.

"I *will* wee-wee on their moufs," Lumino assured the apprentice.

Ronan laughed quietly. "Shh, little prince. You will get your chance, but now we must be stealthy."

As Ronan sneaked around them, and Scarro searched the crowd for signs of the sixth chief, the shamans continued to round up demons. They had taken down fifty-seven by the time Malík made an unsettling observation. "Xersek, have you noticed?"

"Noticed what?" the exorcist asked, as he stuffed another disembodied demon into the lantern.

"None of them are moving."

A chill went down the exorcist's spine, as he looked around them at the more than fifty gnomes they'd saved. He crouched down, searching the nearest body for signs of life. He looked up, horrified, with a shake of his head, moving on to the next body, while Malík held the other demons at bay with the threat of his staff.

Malík nearly tripped over one of the bodies, then looked down with recognition. He knelt beside it, his staff and eyes still aimed at the remaining demons, and felt for a pulse, finding none. He stood. "This cannot be." He looked to Xersek, whose countenance had fallen dramatically. "I've found King Soma. Unfortunately … he is dead."

Xersek answered morosely. "They are all dead, Malík. What have I done? I've made some mistake. This shouldn't be happening."

Both shamans noticed the emboldened state of the remaining demons. They knew that the shamans' strategy had been compromised.

Malík reached down and removed the crown from King Soma's head. "I will take this back to Infractus, along with his son, good king. Rest easy in the knowledge that your son will rule Tribe Riven well."

"Malík …" Xersek was backing up.

"What do you suggest?" Malík enquired of the exorcist.

"Where is the child?" Xersek asked.

"Ronan has him," Scarro said, having found his way to the shamans. "I'm still trying to find the last chief."

"Scarro!" Ronan called from a little ways off. "I've found him."

Scarro and the shamans turned to see a mostly skeletal demon swinging at Ronan with an enormous sword.

Too close to get a good position to fire an energy bolt at the monster, Ronan lifted his sword to defend, but was off balance from the moment he raised his weapon, for carrying

Lumino in his other arm. Forced to hold the sword in his weaker left hand, while instinctively holding the child in his stronger arm, it was not more than an instant before the attacking demon had knocked the sword from Ronan's hand altogether, leaving the warrior's apprentice defenseless.

The demon's skull turned, and its bleeding, empty eye sockets stared directly at little Lumino, as it kept Ronan trapped within reach of the enormous sword. "If we will not have Prince Infractus, we no longer have need of his son … *son.*" The demon raised the sword and brought it down hard, determined to strike the child a fatal blow.

"No!!!" Ronan, though he had no sword, moved without a thought to protect the child, pushing him to the side and raising his right arm to block the blow, and, while he did save the child, the unforgiving blade took his arm off cleanly at the shoulder. "*Scarro!!!!*"

"Ronan! No!" Scarro ran to his apprentice, attacking the demon chief so fiercely that the supernatural monster didn't have time to think before Scarro had severed its head, grabbed a torch, and lit the bony carcass on fire.

As Malík and Xersek dealt with the escaping demon spirit, Scarro fell to the ground and held Ronan in his arms.

The youth was shivering, his skin had gone pale as snow. He was bleeding to death.

"Ronan, be brave."

"Scarro …"

"Don't try to talk, Ronan."

"No … I'm … not finished, Scarro. I'm not finished. It can't end here … It won't. I'm a poet."

"What? Ronan, be still." He hugged the young warrior tightly, fighting back tears to no avail.

"My pen name … Ronan the Left-Handed." Through his shivering, Ronan managed a laugh.

The demons began closing in around them, further emboldened by the scene and the fresh scent of blood.

Malík scooped up Prince Lumino.

The demon chief who had been deliberately spared spoke, "Now you see what happens when you remove us from our hosts, exorcist! … *excorcist.* Will you kill all of these innocent bodies, just to save one child … *child?*"

"Scarro …" Ronan weakly whispered.

"It's the call of Nubus, young warrior," Scarro answered through silent, painful tears. "You must go now. Cross the Great Horizon, and greet the gods with honor."

"Uh … I think I'll pull through … old man."

"Ronan, quiet yourself. You must go bravely into Nubus' arms."

"You first …"

The demons closed in.

Malík frantically searched his satchel for something.

"Ronan …" Scarro searched for the words.

"We're out of time," Xersek barked out sharply, circling the five of them with a fine powder, as the demons leapt all around them for the kill. He stamped his staff on the ground, and a blinding light engulfed them within the circle.

The demons pounced, but they landed on an empty circle where their prey had once been. They looked around, dumbfounded.

The chief growled. "Bah! Shamans! … *Shamans.*" He picked up Ronan's severed arm and began sucking the blood from the rending wound.

8
A Secret Room

Suddenly finding himself in the dark, Scarro froze instinctively. "What happened?"

A soft, violet glow revealed the Demon Stone and Xersek in the darkness. "We are relatively safe, for the moment. I had to teleport us out of there, so that we could rethink our strategy."

Malík's voice spoke out of the darkness, "Excellent vantage point."

Scarro followed the voice, as his eyes adjusted, and he noted a subtle light coming through the wall beside the face of the older shaman. "Malík?"

"Yes … Ah! There it is!" Malík held something white in his hand, barely visible in the light. He walked from the window and allowed the red glow of his staff's jewel to light his way. He found the wounded apprentice, and the child Lumino was sitting beside him looking forlorn and holding the young hero's remaining hand.

"What is it?" Scarro asked. He looked at the silent body. "He's gone, isn't he, Malík?"

"No," Malík said. "And neither will he be going."

"You make him better?" Lumino asked, hopefully. "You make him arm grow back?"

Malík sadly shook his head. "No, my prince, I am afraid I can only do so much. Growing back arms is not within my power." Malík knelt down beside the fallen hero, holding his upper body in his lap. He peeled away the remains of Ronan's shirt and began to rub the chalky substance in his hand over the youth's mutilated shoulder.

"Ow … Scarro …"

Scarro knelt beside them. "I'm here, Ronan." He nodded to Lumino, who released Ronan's hand so that his mentor could take it in his. "Be strong."

"Have I survived it?"

"Hmm," Malík answered. "Not yet, my tremendously brave young friend."

"I still hurt. I'm so cold." He shivered visibly.

Malík studied the area to which he had applied the treatment. "Good. The medicine is working. The wound is no longer bleeding, but he's lost a *great* deal of blood, and I had to use the entire bar of bloodpaste to stop it." He looked to Scarro and Xersek in turn. "If we do not get him back to Tribe Qadash very soon, he *will* die, and there will be nothing that I can do for him."

"I'm not going anywhere," Ronan insisted, through his shivering. "Maybe not even back to the tribe. It hurts too much. Oh, Malík, it hurts!"

"Shh," Malík moved a rebellious lock of sandy-brown hair away from the boy's eyes with his hand. "We must remain quiet, or be discovered. Swallow this." He removed a small vial from his pouch, pulled out the cork, and poured it into Ronan's mouth.

The apprentice's knee-jerk reaction to the foul-tasting concoction was to try to spit it out immediately, but Malík had anticipated this and gripped him under the chin, holding a hand over his mouth, and forcing the young gnome to swallow.

"What was it?" Scarro asked.

"Well," Malík returned the cork to the bottle and the bottle to his pouch, "it won't stop the pain, but it *will* stop him *caring* that he's in pain." The shaman smirked. "There may be other side effects as well. But not to worry."

"Ah," Scarro said. "Thank you, Malík."

The shaman nodded with a smile. "I'm only glad I thought to bring a bar of bloodpaste before I left home tonight."

Scarro looked to the exorcist. "Nice place you found. Where are we, exactly?"

"Yes," Xersek said. "I noticed these upper chambers when we first entered the main room. I saw the dark windows and took note. It's my policy to always have an exit strategy, even if the plan goes to pot."

Malík removed a bandage from his satchel and dressed Ronan's shoulder as well as he could, pleased to note that the young gnome was already falling under the influence of the medicine enough that he did not seem troubled by the attention to his wound.

Once the bandage was firmly in place, wrapped around Ronan's shoulder and chest, Malík gently laid the boy back down. He nodded to Scarro, having given the injured apprentice all the comfort that he could.

Certain there was nothing more they could do for him, Scarro gave Ronan's hand an affectionate squeeze, then laid it down over the youth's chest. He stood, leaving Ronan to rest, and went to the window that Malík had been standing beside a moment before. He looked down upon the demons, who were fairly bewildered by the sudden departure of their enemies. He turned to Xersek. "So why not just teleport us out of these caverns altogether if you have that sort of magic?"

"Teleportation is a tricky, dangerous business, Scarro. However, the risk of it in this instance outweighed the risk of *not* teleporting by a significant degree. Besides, we aren't finished here. We have still other gnomes to save from the hold of the Demons of the Blood."

Scarro left the window, returning to the gentle glow of the shamans' staves. "But how? All of them that we *did* try to save have died."

"About that," Malík asked Xersek, "what do you think went wrong?"

Xersek looked down with a shake of his head. "I don't know. We could look at the book again, but I really don't think I missed anything." He nodded to himself. "Still … I *must* have." He reached into his pocket, but was stopped by a quiet, somber voice.

"No, Xersek, you will not find the answer in your books this time."

While the shaman already knew who was speaking, it was a tremendous surprise to Scarro. "Bin Riven! But, I thought you had died."

The form of Bin Riven smiled affectionately at his friend, and Scarro noticed a slight glow to the gnome, and the fact that he could see the wall right through him. "Oh," Scarro said.

"I told you he sees ghosts," Ronan said from the floor, with a slight slur and a giggle. "I don't see anybody." He turned to Lumino. "Do you?" Without waiting for an answer, he turned to no one at all, and asked, "Do you?" He laughed. "Of course you don't! You're not anybody. I'm asking nobody a question! Shh! I want to hear his answer." He laughed again.

Ignoring the drugged apprentice, Scarro addressed the spirit in their midst, "Bin, I'm so sorry. We would have saved you if we'd known how."

"Don't worry about that, Scarro. There was nothing you could have done about it. It's part of the demons' curse. None can be possessed by the Demons of the Blood and live. The minute they take hold of you, your blood begins to boil within your veins. It's why their eyes and ears bleed. All those gnomes, down in the great chamber, are already dead."

"My grandpa?" Lumino asked, a whimper in his voice.

"Oh, he sees them too!" Ronan said. "That's okay. I don't feel left out. I'll just go back to barely not dying. I'm a poet anyway. I'll just dream things that none of *you* can see." He grinned and shut his eyes, drifting off to not-quite-sleep.

"Lumino," King Soma said softly, as he materialized in ghostly form out of the darkness beside Bin, "there is no such thing as death. Only a change."

"Grandpa!"

"I will always be with you, Lumino. Just … in another dimension."

"Is there really nothing we can do?" Malík asked the spirits, no stranger to such apparitions himself. "There are more than seventy possessed bodies down there, and more than fifty already dead."

"No, Malík," Soma corrected, "they are *all* already dead, as Bin said. Trying to save them will get you all killed as well. It's a trap, this idea that you can save them; a trick of the demons. But if the blood is pouring from their eyes and ears, their blood has boiled, and their spirits have departed."

He looked to his grandson, "Lumino, I have to go now, but I'll be watching you grow up. I'll be right there with you and with your father and mother. I'm proud of you. You're being very brave. When you get home, tell your father, I'm proud of him too. I know he'll be a fine king, better than I ever was myself."

"Okay, Grandpa. Bye-bye now," Lumino said, with what little understanding he had of his grandfather's new situation.

The ghostly king chuckled merrily. "Bye-bye, Lumino." He looked Scarro in the eyes. "And that is how we say goodbye." The king vanished, a smile still on his lips.

Lumino patted Ronan on the face, jarring the youth from his reverie. "My grandpa had do go to unudder umenshun, but you … you can stay here with me now, okay?"

Ronan smiled at the toddler. "Of course, my prince. As you command." He winked. "I have things to do now anyway."

Scarro shook his head, amazed at Ronan's disposition. "He's raving." He looked to Malík, desperately. "What can he possibly *do*? He's been destroyed by those things. Even if he lives, no one who has been so mutilated can be made a warrior in full. His life is over. He served gallantly, and he was robbed of a warrior's death."

"There's so much more to life than death, Scarro," the ghost of Bin Riven assured him, clearly amused. "Unfortunately, some of us must die before we see this. I, for one, valued my time in the flesh. I died, knowing I had left things well with my wife and our two sons. I missed nothing. I held them every chance I had, and I laughed with them every day that I was with them. My life was worth something. The horror of my passing is far outshined by the brightness of my life. I have no regrets."

Xersek spoke at last. "It's not normally so easy for a spirit to come through, and yet here there have been two who just appear and carry on conversations as though nothing should be stopping them. What's your secret?" His eyes narrowed suspiciously, as he waited for an answer.

Bin continued to smile, and he shrugged. "It's this place. There's an energy about it. Something in the walls themselves. The Lost Tribe must have been *very* in touch with the spirit world."

Xersek nodded, satisfied. "Yes, this place has a presence about it." He considered. "Many presences."

"Precisely," Bin said. "Now, I must go. It's not really *right* for me to be here like this. I just wanted to tell you that you've done all you could for those gnomes down there. End the threat that remains, and go home to your lives." His eyes turned to Scarro. "Savor all the time you have with your families." To the wounded apprentice, whose eyes had closed once more, he said, "And Ronan, I can already smell that blueberry pie." Still with a happy air about him, the spirit of Bin Riven vanished back into the ether.

Thinking the idea had been his own, Ronan sat up suddenly, eyes wide. "Oh, yes! Blueberry pie! I get a reward for my return home after all!" He noticed the two shamans and his teacher looking at him sadly. "All right, everyone needs to stop looking at me as if I'm ruined!"

"Ronan," Scarro started. "You've been drugged. For your own good. You may not realize—"

"That I'll never be a warrior now? That I go home a cripple? That I will bear, to no end, the pity of my fellows?" He laughed. "You are the one who doesn't realize, old man, that I can do so much more. I told you, I'm a poet. I write sonnets, I write little epics, and someday, I shall write grand epics! With my left hand! I write love poems! I love blueberry pie, and I love not dying! And I love Moonie-Su! I walked with her, in her secret garden, with only the stars to spy upon us! She led me there and gave me her most precious flower. I took that flower, and I have carried it in my heart ever since! I love you, Moonie-Su! Oh, Moonie-Su! Blueberry Pie! Flower of love!"

"I wuv flowers," said Lumino.

Ronan giggled stupidly at the child's declaration.

"Dear gods!" said Scarro, gruffly. "So he is a poet."

Scarro was about to say more, but he was preempted by the abrupt lapse of his apprentice, from avid declarations of his love, into sleep and gentle snoring.

"It's the potion," said Malík. "Better that he sleeps."

"Why did King Soma's ghost say what he said?" Scarro asked.

"Which part?" Xersek prompted.

"He looked me right in the eyes and said, 'That is how we say goodbye.' "

Malík considered, a shrewd look upon his face. "I suppose he must have been with us a while. Perhaps he and Bin have overheard some of our conversations. Bin did seem to know about Ronan's love for blueberry pie. They were clearly paying attention to our conversation about how these two fathers say goodbye to their sons."

Scarro stared at Ronan, sleeping peacefully, in spite of the great wound at his shoulder. The sight nearly moved the hardened warrior back to tears. "He's so … *hopeful.* If that were me, lying there, instead of him … If I'd lost a limb in battle and survived. I would be … I would be finished. I

would be like Meso No'tall, the once great warrior who now drinks in taverns at all hours, after losing an eye and a leg and being driven from the warrior life. I would be worse. I would drink myself to death. But Ronan! Ronan is perfectly at peace, dreaming of some girl and going home to blueberry pie and the life of a simple poet. He's not even hit a snag, aside from the fact that he's— that he *was* right-handed."

His eyes searched the faces of the two shamans, who only listened to him serenely. He searched their eyes for answers, but the only answers he heard were already within his heart. "My father told me how harsh the warrior life was, how unforgiving, just as I've taught Jono, just as my entire line from Lorok down has done. I thought I was strengthening Jono, but seeing this now, all this hope built on blueberry pie in the midst of demon corpses, ghosts, and a severed limb. It's more than any words could have revealed. If that were me, or any of Lorok's line, lying there with only one arm, any one of us would have crumbled. But there he sleeps, peacefully dreaming of blueberry pie, because that's what *his* father promised him. I always thought that true strength came from acceptance, but here the stronger gnome is a seventeen-year-old who is full of hopes and half-mad, poetic dreams.

"Maybe … Maybe there is more than one sort of 'demon of the blood.' Maybe some come in the form of the darkness handed down from a jaded father to his impressionable son, piercing his dreams with a cold reality that, perhaps, does not need to be. Why can my line not have been as Ronan's?"

"Why not, indeed, Scarro? Jono is only ten." Malík winked. "After all, Lorok's daughter Nuna, the sister of *your* great-grandfather Tomar, married Boontu Kah, and their great-great-grandson lies there now, teaching you what the blood of Lorok could also be. As it turns out, Lorok's father was a baker himself, and his father the clan patriarch of his day *and* a noted poet. You and Ronan both are born of the blood of Lorok. One of your lines chose to see life as a prelude to death; the other chose blueberry pie."

Scarro shook his head, astonished. "I never knew. I might have been a shaman. Ronan is of the blood of Lorok. All my life, I have believed that the line of Lorok was cursed to die in bloody battle. All my life."

Malík put a hand on Scarro's shoulder. "I have seen the families of our tribe, in all their ups and downs. Sometimes, there are tragedies, yes. Sometimes one after another, as with your own line, but I have never encountered a family 'curse' that wasn't somehow self-inflicted."

Scarro nodded. "I'm going to change this. Jono is a happy, loving boy, like Ronan. He makes me laugh, but I hide it from him. I hide it to make him strong, to harden his spirit. But no more. I will teach Jono the lesson of Ronan, even as I struggle to learn it myself."

"A noble goal, Scarro," Malík said.

"Oh, yes," Xersek agreed sarcastically. "Now that our remarkable journey of self-discovery has ended, perhaps we should all go back to Ronan's and celebrate by stuffing ourselves with these wonderful pies that no one seems to want to shut up about. *Or*, we could get back to the matter at hand."

Scarro grinned at the shaman. "Why so grim, Xersek? Of course, let us return to these monsters who have killed so many innocent gnomes this day."

"What do you suggest, Xersek?" Malík asked. "We are only three, and we must also protect Ronan and Lumino.

We can't walk back in, as we did before. Any thoughts of talking our way out of this are futile at this point."

Xersek nodded. "We *must* destroy the bodies and trap the demons. There are seventy-seven left, by my count. And we must leave the chief alive until the last. That will be the challenge."

"Why is that?" Scarro asked. "I wondered, when Malík said we had to leave one alive."

Xersek explained, "As long as the demons are trapped in a bloodline, they cannot jump into one of us. We must leave the last chief trapped in a body until we have mopped up his underlings."

"But wouldn't it be all the same if we left an underling instead of a chief?" asked the warrior.

"No. There was a point made in *The Necromancy of Gothos* that if the demon chiefs are all dealt with, while any of their underlings are still free, the underlings become chiefs themselves and gain all the abilities of such, able to jump into whatever bloodline they come across as they like. According to the book, there was once only one chief. Now there are six. We don't want to make it seven."

"I see your point," Scarro said. "So what do we do?"

Xersek took a purposeful breath and let it out, slowly. He studied sleeping Ronan and the toddler prince who seemed to be standing guard over him. "One of you get the child to stay calm. It can't be me. I'm not so good with children. I'm too creepy, apparently."

At this, both Malík and Scarro tried to hide their grins.

"Ehem … Thank you for not arguing," Xersek muttered grumpily. "After that, we simply teleport back in and start swinging at everything that moves, aside from the last chief. Fortunately, he's a big, nasty skeleton with a wobbly head and a sword, so he's easy to keep an eye on. Our only hope, long shot that it is, will be to appear suddenly and kill as many of them as we can without being killed ourselves."

Scarro shook his head. "This is why shamans aren't generals."

"Better idea, Scarro?" Xersek asked pointedly.

The warrior thought for only a moment, then frowned. "No. It's a mad solution to a mad problem. In our present state, there is no reasonable alternative."

"Nope," called Ronan, not bothering to move as he spoke. "But you could help yourselves by making it less overwhelming. Instead of all of you going in to kill seventy-six, each of you should make your goal to kill a third of them. Scarro and Malík, kill twenty-five, and keep count. Xersek, twenty-six. Kill, count, and you'll be through before you know it. Then only the chief remains."

"Very good point, Ronan," Scarro praised. "I feel less overwhelmed already."

"Hey, old man," Ronan said amiably, "I could have been a general."

"Yes," Scarro agreed. "And now you'll be a poet, and I will be just as proud of you." To the shamans, he said, "With the element of surprise, and your staves' magic, we really might pull it off. Especially if you can teleport us near Ronan's sword. Then we all have a powerful magical weapon to fight these demons with from a distance."

The shamans nodded their agreement.

Scarro walked over and knelt back down beside Ronan, who had again fallen asleep abruptly. He met the solemn gaze of the little prince at Ronan's side. "Lumino, Ronan is my apprentice. He is very dear to me. Can I count on you to stay here with him and watch over him, while we're taking care of things down there?"

The boy nodded. "Ronan potect me. Now I potect him."

Scarro nodded with a gentle smile, then stood to rejoin the shamans. "Ready when you are."

Xersek cast the circle of powder around them. "Then the time is now!"

As the exorcist raised his staff, Malík readied his own weapon for battle, and Scarro drew his sword.

Xersek's staff hit the ground, and, in a brilliant flash, they vanished, trading the safety of the secret upper room for the terrors of the supernatural monsters waiting down below.

9
The Final Stand

The two shamans and the warrior appeared in the great chamber and instantly sprang into action. Scarro grabbed Firebolt, where it had fallen, and blasted whatever demon came into his sight. He also took the lantern that Xersek handed him, to man the door for the two shamans.

Malík, no longer holding back, now that there was no chance of saving the possessed gnomes, used his magic to engulf whichever demons he found in his path in flames, then immediately trapped them in the light of his staff and guided them into the lantern.

Xersek no longer wasted the time it took to push the demons out of their stolen bodies and adopted a similar tactic to that of Malík, shooting a flame from his staff and forcing the demons to abandon the burning bodies.

As they went, they each kept careful count and a close eye out for the last remaining chief.

In the midst of the battle, a war cry, not belonging to any of them, sounded throughout the great chamber, "I wee-wee on you!"

The heroes all looked up to see young Prince Lumino standing in the window of the secret room, and true to his word, dropping his pants and taking deliberate aim at the demons.

"I wee-wee on your moufs!"

Careful not to lose focus, Scarro saw, from the corner of his eye, a laughing Ronan grabbing the boy with his one arm and pulling him down from the window and back into the now not-so-secret room. In spite of the fact that he was drenched in the blood of countless gnomes who had been the victims of unspeakable evil, Scarro laughed.

The battle raged, but was over quickly. In a matter of minutes, the shamans and the warrior found themselves catching their breath, as Scarro closed the lantern door on the last demon in the room. "That's it then?" Scarro asked tentatively. "We must have gotten the chief by mistake."

"I doubt that," Xersek said. "What's your count?"

"I got eighteen," Scarro said.

"Twenty," from Malík.

"I got thirty-eight." Xersek confessed, grimly. When he noticed the stares of his friends, he added. "Well, I *am* an exorcist."

"So, where is the chief?" Malík asked, looking around the room cautiously.

"I don't know," Xersek said. "But we must get to the young ones, before he does. Especially if he saw that crazy prince's … *episode.*"

"You're right," Scarro said, wasting no more time. He led the way, at a run, to a staircase he had discovered during the battle.

When the trio reached the secret room, they found Ronan sitting up, holding the prince back from the window with a smile. "Success?" he asked.

"Not yet," Xersek said. "We seem to have misplaced one."

"I'm at least relieved for the moment," said Malík. "I had feared if we accidentally killed his body, the chief would have taken another host."

Scarro went to stand by Ronan, putting a hand to the boy's pale forehead, showing his concern silently. "That's a fun prospect. Ronan looks fine, and so does Prince Lumino."

"Aside from the obvious, old man," Ronan said. "But I think that potion is wearing off." He winced in pain.

"He couldn't have taken either of the boys," said Xersek, nodding towards Malík, "nor either one of us. He could only have targeted someone with offspring, and Scarro was with us. I say the demon is still in his stolen body. Well, his stolen skeleton. Whatever it is."

"Correct you are, shaman ... *shaman*."

All eyes turned towards the entrance to the room, where stood the last demon chief. No sooner had his presence registered, than the skeleton collapsed where it stood, its head rolling back down the stairs without a hint of life.

Malík and Xersek, quick as they had been to react, found themselves burning an already empty vessel, as the disembodied demon itself flew forth towards Scarro.

Surprised by the move, the shamans turned to stop the demon, only to face their greatest fear.

Scarro picked up little Lumino, then coldly put the cutting edge of Firebolt to the toddler's throat. "Foolish shaman, a lone chief can move freely from one body to the next, whether it's body has been destroyed or not. Add that to your inadequate book … *book*.

"You may have defeated us, but your little one and the lame one will die before you trap me in that lantern … *lantern*. Not to mention," he shrugged, indicating Scarro's body, "*this* one, who is already dead … *dead*."

Xersek took aim, but hesitated.

Already faint, Ronan fell back in horror at the inescapable fate of his mentor. He tried to stand, but his legs failed him. "No! He isn't bleeding. It's not too late!"

"He's right," Malík said. "Scarro! Fight it! You have a magic within you that is rare! You have the powers of a shaman! Fight it! Push the demon *out*!"

A trickle of blood fell from the warrior's eye. "Malík … help me … me … *me*!"

"It's too late, Malík," Xersek said flatly. "He's already dead."

"No," Malík insisted. "He can fight this. Look!"

Xersek noticed the sword had moved away from Lumino. "Scarro?" he asked.

Scarro, visibly struggling to take control of his own body, released his grip on Lumino, who landed on his feet and scurried over to Ronan as quickly as he could.

"Xersek!" Scarro pleaded. "I have to have more time … *time*!" Blood began to drip from his ears and his nose. "Jono can't wind up like me! You have to give me more time with my son! … *son*. Please! … *Please*."

Suddenly, Scarro cried out, and then his voice was joined by another, as two agonized voices cried out in pain from his body.

The demon was no sooner forcibly ejected from Sacrro's body than it was caught in the light of both shamans' staves and ushered into its new prison within the magic lantern.

"He did it!" Malík shouted. "Scarro, I knew you had the power to fight it!" He paused, looking down at the warrior, who had fallen to the floor. "Scarro?" He knelt down and rolled the warrior over.

Scarro's blood-rimmed eyes stared back at him lifelessly.

Xersek put a hand on his friend's shoulder. "I'm so sorry, Malík."

Ronan found just enough strength to will himself across the floor, over to Scarro. Without a word, he wrapped his one arm around his beloved mentor, and he wept upon his chest.

Lumino ran to Xersek and hugged him tightly around the leg. Xersek, unused to such things from children, got over his surprise and picked the boy up. He may have been strong for a three-year-old, but he had still seen far too many terrible things this day. Xersek looked to the ether. "Scarro, my friend, I'll see what I can do."

Malík held Ronan, until the tears had taken all of the lad's remaining strength, then the shaman leaned over to close the fallen warrior's eyes, and he picked Ronan up in his arms and carried him out of the caverns of the Lost Tribe, into the cold, dark night from whence they had come. "A poet, indeed," he whispered to the sleeping youth. "I look forward to seeing just what you become."

10
The Heroes' Return

By the time the four gnomes arrived back at the caverns of Tribe Qadash, the sun had risen, which was no use to a nocturnal creature such as Digger. They found a shady spot to tie him down and entered the caverns of Tribe Qadash, making their way towards the section of the caverns that belonged to Clan Jinto.

Malík stopped a messenger on the way and sent word to Prince Infractus of Tribe Riven that his son had been saved and that Xersek would be returning with him. He also sent the terrible news that King Soma was dead, as were all of the gnomes who had been taken over by the now vanquished Demons of the Blood. The messenger left for Tribe Riven at once, and the shamans, each carrying a young one, made their way as quickly as they could to the home of Melendie Jinto.

At the door, they smelled breakfast cooking, and Malík loathed himself for what he must now put Melendie and Jono through; though, he hoped for Jono at least, things would not be quite as bad, if Xersek was as true to his word as he expected him to be.

He put Ronan down on his feet. "Feeling better?"

Ronan nodded. "Yes, thank you, Malík. I'm just weak."

"A good breakfast will fix that, and I must insist that you eat, in spite of your grief." Malík had tended Ronan's wound anew with supplies stored in the carriage atop Xersek's armadillo. The young gnome was still in pain, but he was tolerating it. Malík had no doubt that Ronan would make something of himself as a poet, or whatever he put his mind to being.

To Xersek, he said, "I will console Melendie as well as I can, then I will go to Ronan's family and tell them what has happened. I'd rather not shock them with the sight of him without some warning."

He winked at the boy playfully. "Then I'll go to the home of Moonie-Su Tikvah. I'm sure she and her parents will want to come and see Ronan too."

"Hold, shaman! After all the blood and the entire arm I lost in this mad quest of yours, you would have me meet the parents?" Ronan laughed. "Do it. It is time. And tell my father to bring—"

"Blueberry pie!" the shamans finished his sentence in unison.

"Yes, we know," Xersek said. "Moonie-Su and blueberry pie. That's all you talk about when you're on Malík's potions."

Ronan laughed, in spite of the pain he felt in both his shoulder and the very depths of his heart.

Malík took a deep breath. "Well, I suppose it's time."

He knocked three times upon the door with his staff.

Melendie answered with a bright smile. "The heroes return!" She took in the shocking sight of her husband's apprentice. "Ronan! Oh, Ronan!" She hugged him fiercely and ushered him inside, leaving the shamans at the door.

Jono came into the entry room then and gasped at the sight of Ronan.

Ronan grinned at the boy. "I did promise your mother no more than two."

Little Lumino ran past Melendie then to stay by Ronan's side. "He potect me. Now, I potect him," he said.

Melendie smiled at the boy. "Prince Lumino, I presume." She bowed. "It is an honor to have you in our home. Jono, take them into the kitchen and get them some breakfast."

"Were there monsters?" Jono asked excitedly.

"There were indeed," Xersek answered from the doorway. "But they are a threat no more."

"I wee-weed on their moufs," Lumino assured Jono.

Jono laughed. "*What?*"

Smiling, Melendie went back to the doorway. "Come in. Ak'ten's in the kitchen having breakfast as we speak." Sadly, she asked, "What happened? With Ronan?" She noticed the sorrow painted on the faces of the two shamans. Her countenance fell, and her skin went white with dread. "Where's Scarro?"

Jono watched, as his mother's face fell into her hands and she began to sob. A darkness crossed his own face then, as he began to comprehend what had happened, and he turned, stoically, and walked into his room. Just as his father had done so many years ago, upon the death of his own father.

11
The Last Demon

Time stood still for Jono, until his door slowly creaked open. He remained seated on his bed, facing the wall. Somehow he knew it was the shaman from Tribe Riven at his door. He determined to be strong, like his father would have wanted. Though there was a slight tremble in his voice, he managed to hide it well. "My father is dead, isn't he?"

"It's complicated," Xersek answered, "and I've a promise to keep. May I come in?"

Jono turned, struggling to hold back the tears that were welling up in his sad, brown eyes, but determined to do it for his father, who had warned him that this would happen, time and again. He nodded, the muscles of his face struggling to hold back any sign of emotion. He was the man of the house now. He would live and die in battle someday, just as his father had done. He must remain strong.

Xersek entered, and he removed an oddly shaped rock from the deep inside pocket of his robe. "Your father is among the bravest gnomes that I have ever met. The demons took possession of him, tried to use him to kill little Lumino. Your father used his inborn magic to force the demon out of his body. I have never, in all my time as a demonologist, seen a possessed gnome perform an exorcism on himself."

"Inborn magic?" Jono asked.

"Yes. Your father might have been a shaman, as it turns out, but your grandfather refused to allow it. And you, young Jono, could even be a healer yourself, if *you* should allow it."

Jono looked away, a tear finally escaping his eye. "I … I am to be a warrior. I have no time for things such as healing."

Xersek nodded. "Your father made some discoveries, before he died, Jono. Discoveries that he would like to share with you now."

"But how can he?" Jono asked, still fighting the further fall of tears. "He's dead."

Xersek chuckled. "It's a matter of perspective, I suppose. I made him a promise, before I left the caverns in which he made his final stand, and I always keep my word."

"What promise?"

"One more day with you," Scarro answered for himself, appearing beside the shaman.

"Father!" Jono's face contorted, fighting harder than ever not to let his feelings show.

"Let them flow, Son. There is great healing strength in tears, just as there is in laughter."

Jono needed no further prompting, letting loose all the tears that his eyes could produce.

Xersek sat beside him on the bed, a comforting arm around his shoulders.

At last, Jono looked up to his father, whose ghostly arms, he knew, would never hold him again. "Why just one more day, Father? Why not ask for a year? Why not ask for always? I want you to stay!"

Scarro smiled at his son, his eyes filled with love, appreciating that Jono would have him stay forever if it were possible.

Xersek answered for him. "It is not a natural thing for spirits to spend very much time interacting with the living. But we discovered, in these strange caverns where we fought the Demons of the Blood, that the walls themselves had a property that resonated with the spirits around us." He handed the rock to Jono. "Hold onto this, Jono. It was a loose stone I found as we made our departure. I pulled it from the wall. It gives your father extra spirit energy, so that he can stay here, in plain sight, for quite a while. But he must leave you at sunset, to go where he must go. After which, he will always be near you, watching what you do with your life."

Xersek stood. "I will leave you to it, Scarro." He smiled. "There is yet one more demon left for you to slay."

Scarro nodded his thanks, as the shaman left the room and closed the door behind him.

Jono stood. "I won't disappoint you, Father. I will be more serious. I will be hard and strong. I will die in glorious battle as you did, as your father did, as his father—"

Scarro laughed, and the alien sight and sound of it stopped Jono mid-sentence. "Father?"

"I wish these arms could hug you, Jono! But I have to tell you something that I never did let you know. You make me laugh. Sometimes, when I am alone, thinking of home, I remember something silly that you said, and I laugh out loud and grow stronger, thinking of returning to you."

"I'm sorry—"

"No! My wonderful son, I am not scolding you. I am *proud* of you. You are a healer, with your very presence, you heal and make people happy. You could learn to do more, to use magic, if you wanted to, just as the shaman said.

"I learned, nearly too late, that there is far more to the line of Lorok than living a hard life and dying in darkness. The wonders and joys of life outshine all of the hardships of death. I was wrong to teach you otherwise. I was wrong, Son. Do you understand?"

Jono shook his head, bewildered. "Father … I'm confused. Do you not want me to be a warrior, like you?"

"I want you to be Jono. Be whatever you feel *called* to be; a warrior, if you like, but anything else will do." Scarro closed his eyes. "May the gods give me the strength to undo all of the damage that I have done, in this last day that we have together." He opened his eyes again and smiled at Jono.

"You seem … happy."

"I am happy, Jono! Because death is not real, and I am here with you, and I will always be with you and your mother, even when you can't see me. I'm just on another plane. But it's no less real. And, Jono, when I look in on you, I don't want you to be like me, or my father, or his father. I want you to be the same Jono I think of when I am away from home. I want you to be happy. I want your life to be filled with love and laughter. I want you never to fear death or think on it, because you are far too busy living your life and relishing the time you have with friends and loved ones. Sing and dance. Tell foolish jokes that make all around you smile. Be a bright star in the dark night around you, no matter how bad things may seem."

"Father," Jono smiled in spite of his previous resolve, "is this really you?"

"More than it ever was in life, Jono. I have been given the gift of telling you the very last lesson I learned. The greatest lesson of my whole life, that I almost failed to pass on to you. You see, the demon of *our* blood has always been this morbid obsession with death and only the hardships of a warrior's life. This is the thing that really took my life, and all of our lives back to the son of Lorok. None of us have ever defeated this family curse that we placed upon ourselves, but you can, Jono. You can stamp out this evil now and pass it on no more. And, I tell you as a father who is already so proud of you that my heart could burst, nothing would make me prouder than to have sired the one who will finally end our curse."

"But how do I fight it, Father?"

"Well," Scarro said, a sly twinkle in his eyes, "I'll show you." He turned around for a moment, Jono waiting eagerly for the lesson. When he abruptly turned back around, his fingers were in his mouth and nose, pulling them back into a ridiculous face.

Jono jumped back, as his father made ludicrous wailings and spun around in mid air, lolling his tongue back and forth like a fool. Suddenly, the boy laughed, forgetting that his father was a ghost at all. "I can do it, Father! I can kill our curse! Like this!" He made his own fantastic face, and his father laughed in turn. It was a high pitched laughter, a joyous sound, and Jono felt whole just hearing it.

Together, they played games, they told foolish jokes and traded more wild faces, they told each other stories, they spoke of hopes and dreams. They spent the rest of the day together in merriment, shining like great stars in the darkness of the world around them; and for the rest of that day, and every day thereafter, Jono laughed.

Selections from the Line of Sypho Jinto

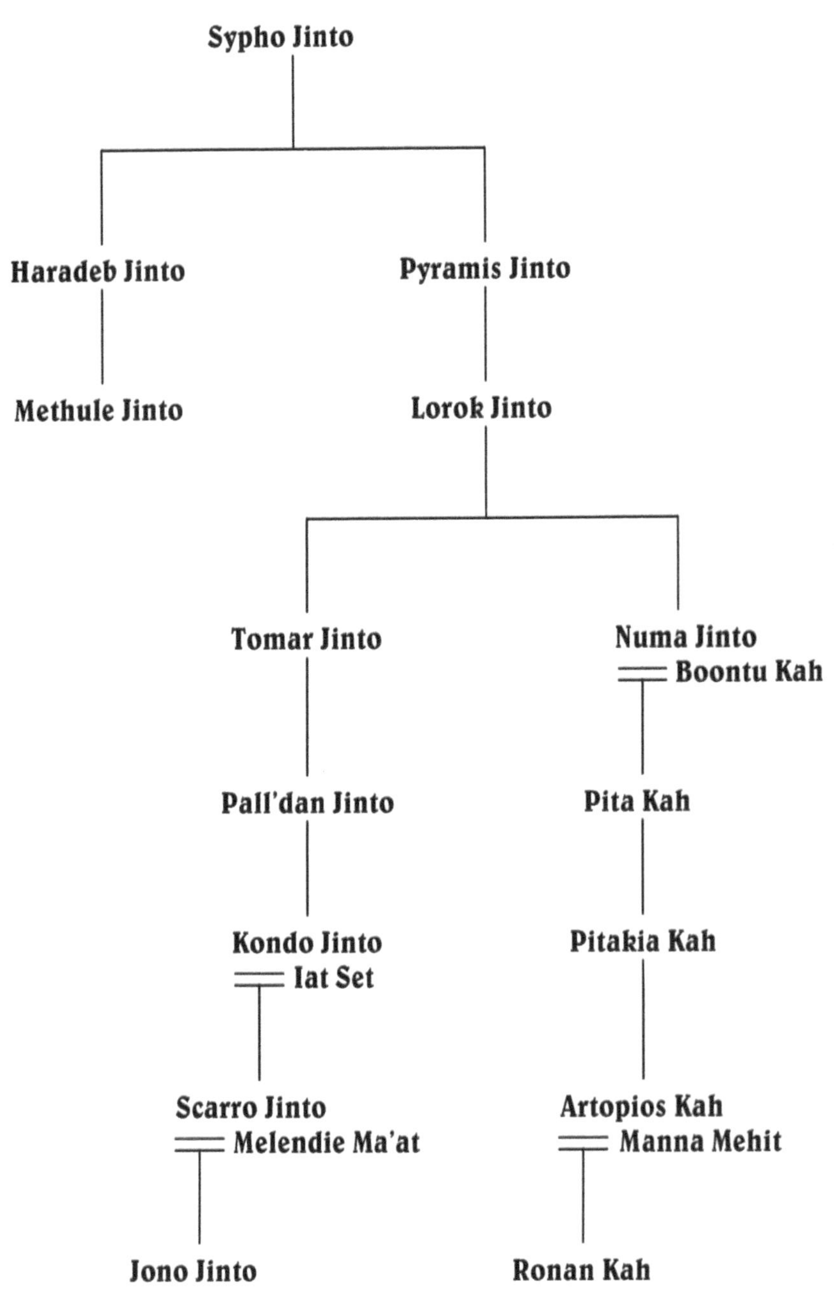

Selections from the Line of Adama Riven

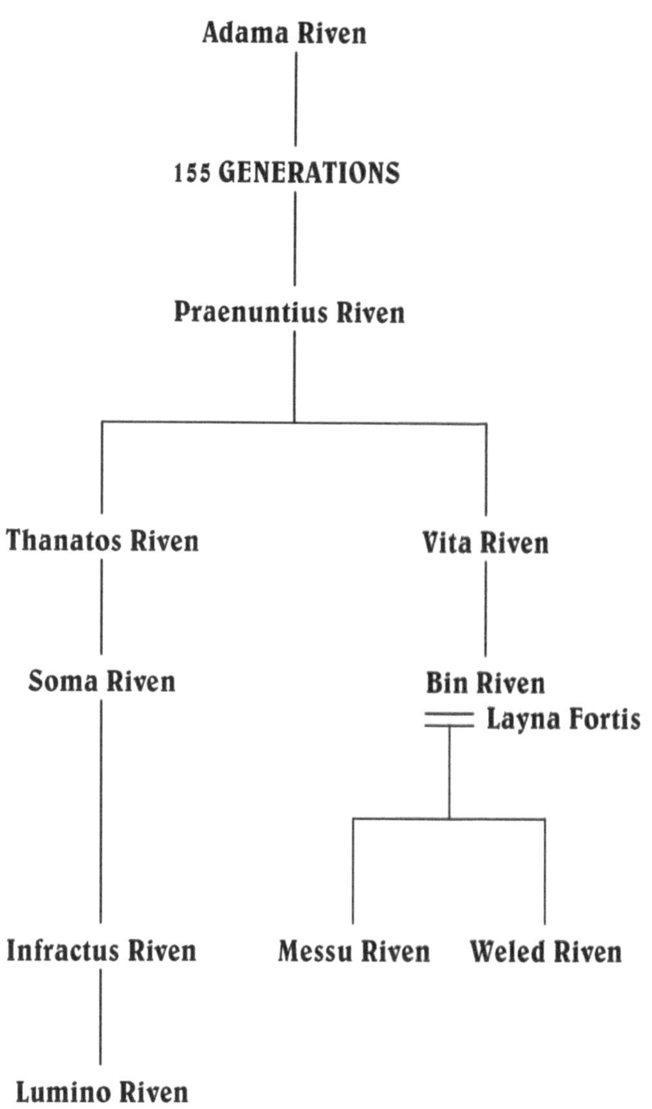

www.ingramcontent.com/pod-product-compliance
Lightning Source LLC
Chambersburg PA
CBHW030814310726
48980CB00006B/491/J

* 9 7 8 1 6 1 8 1 5 1 2 4 7 *